. . . I ran, and it seemed like a mile to the edge of the pond, though it was just past the summer house. But down there at the end of the yard the dark was thick and different—I guess it was the fog that formed over the water. Not a bit of light came from anywhere, so I could barely see the pond. There was a wet, dank smell, and suddenly I thought about all of Edgar Allan Poe's tarns. That pond would have made a great tarn. Without any trouble at all, I could imagine dripping, decaying skeletons rising out of it. . . .

Was that a movement of some kind, over there where the edge of the pond had once caved in?

Was it—Miranda?

Even though she was afraid of the pond, as Eddie said, it might be that ghosts *had* to return and haunt the place where they died, whether they wanted to or not.

There was something moving, down there in the dark. . . .

THE GHOST NEXT DOOR
was originally published by
Harper & Row, Publishers.

Critics' Corner:

". . . a fast-paced first-person story for mystery lovers."
—*A.L.A. Booklist*

"This is a story of the need for love and recognition, and a mystery too, spiced with humor and realism. . . ."
—*Commonweal*

"A thirst for tales of the supernatural will be quenched by Wylly St. John's *The Ghost Next Door*. Well written, fast paced, it's a tantalizing blend of real and unreal about a little girl who seems to be in touch with the ghost of her half sister who died years before. You won't put this book down—but the final answer to its mysteries will be provided by you!"
—*Boston Herald Traveler*

Other Recommendations: Horn Book, National Council of Teachers of English.

About the Author and Illustrator:

WYLLY FOLK ST. JOHN was born near Ehrhardt, South Carolina, and was graduated summa cum laude from the University of Georgia. She is a staff writer for the *Atlanta Journal and Constitution Magazine*. Mrs. St. John has written several books for children, as well as numerous short stories, and was named Georgia Author of the Year in 1968. She and her husband live in Social Circle, Georgia.

TRINA SCHART HYMAN was born in Philadelphia and now lives with her daughter Katrin in Lyme, New Hampshire. She has studied illustration and graphics at the Philadelphia Museum School and the Boston Museum School. Mrs. Hyman has illustrated many books for children.

THE
GHOST
NEXT
DOOR

Wylly Folk St. John

illustrations by Trina Schart Hyman

AN ARCHWAY PAPERBACK
POCKET BOOKS • NEW YORK

THE GHOST NEXT DOOR

Archway Paperback edition published September, 1972

Published by
POCKET BOOKS, a division of Simon & Schuster, Inc.,
630 Fifth Avenue, New York, N.Y.

Archway Paperback editions are distributed in the U.S.
by Simon & Schuster, Inc., 630 Fifth Avenue, New
York, N.Y. 10020, and in Canada by Simon & Schuster
of Canada, Ltd., Richmond Hill, Ontario, Canada.

Standard Book Number: 671-29543-8.
Library of Congress Catalog Card Number: 71-157896.
Text copyright, ©, 1971, by Wylly Folk St. John. Pictures
copyright, ©, 1971, by Trina Schart Hyman. All rights
reserved. This Archway Paperback edition is published by
arrangement with Harper & Row, Publishers, Inc.
Printed in the U.S.A.

This book, with love, is for
the real Lindsey and Eddie and Kirk
and Tammy and Sherry. *And Miranda*.

CONTENTS

1

SHE USED TO
LIVE HERE

I might never have gotten involved with the ghost next door if it hadn't been for Eddie and Kirk, my kid brothers. I don't know why I should feel responsible for those two, but I do. As my best friend Tammy says, blood is thicker than plasma. Her father, Dr. David Greenfield, is a professor at the medical college, so Tammy ought to know—even if he is a psychiatrist instead of a regular doctor.

Tammy and I are both going-on-thirteen, and we'd really be blondes if only our mothers would let us have a color rinse. Eddie's only nine, and Kirk's just six. We don't want them hanging around with us, but sometimes they do anyway.

We live on the edge of a small city in Georgia named Georgetown because George Washington visited here once. Our side of the block has just three houses. The Morrows—that's us—live in the middle one, between the old Alston place and the Greenfields'. We all have great big yards—everybody has around here—and the Greenfields have a tennis court, and Miss Judith Alston has a fish pond way off in the back, past her summer house.

The pond is deep out in the middle—and that's where Miss Judith's little niece Miranda got drowned, a long time ago. Ever since that time, Miss Judith has lived by herself. She's a tall, old-maid lady who believes in ESP and spiritualism and all that stuff, but she likes children—once she gets used to them—especially girls like us. For awhile after Miranda died Miss Judith couldn't stand the sight of a child, I heard Mama say once, because it hurt too much. Seeing any living child made her remember that Miranda wasn't. But that accident happened before I was born.

After we got to know Miss Judith pretty well, she showed Tammy and me the child's picture, which she kept on her piano. It was a tinted photo —Miranda's eyes looked kind of brown-green and her hair was dark brown and sort of floppy. She was only ten. Her chin was pointed and her cheeks were thin. Miss Judith said she was "a faery child," with "a pixie face."

Miss Judith told us how she tried to get in touch with Miranda through a spiritualist group she had joined a few months before—the Georgetown chapter of the American Psychic Society—but she'd had no luck.

"You believe in that stuff, Miss Judith?"

"Well, we don't really know, do we, Lindsey?" she said, sort of wistfully. "If there's the slightest possibility—well, there's no harm in trying—"

I don't believe in it myself, and neither does Tammy, but we didn't tell her that.

Miss Judith was sitting on the piano bench, and the fingers of one hand absent-mindedly picked out a hesitating little tune. Her house is an old-fashioned one with high ceilings, and the notes echoed and seemed to come back from somewhere, very softly.

"What's that you're playing, Miss Judith?" Tammy asked.

She stopped, but the echo went on for a minute. "Was I?" Miss Judith looked at her right hand as if it belonged to somebody else. "Yes, I guess I was. It's a piece called *The Dance of the Fireflies*. Miranda used to practice it over and over. She was going to play it in the recital—that summer."

I knew it wasn't polite to ask questions, but I was dying to know, and she seemed to be in a good mood, so I dared. "Miss Judith, how did Miranda happen to be living with you instead of with her own father and mother?" I had already asked Mama, but she said she'd have to tell me all about it when I got older. Tammy's folks moved here only five years ago, so she couldn't find out either. At least they said they didn't know. When

3

grown-ups say they don't know, you never can be sure whether it's the truth or not.

But Miss Judith told us. "Why, Lindsey, her father and mother were divorced, and she was supposed to live with her father. He is my younger brother, and they lived here in the old family home for several years, while he was connected with that space-research project across the river. He was working for the government, you know, so he had to be away a lot. Especially that spring."

"Yes'm," I said. "I know Dr. Alston is a very famous scientist—my Dad told us that he's a nuclear energy expert. But we've never met him."

"He never has been back," Miss Judith said, and her voice was sad. "He asked for a transfer to Houston. He couldn't bear to be here without Miranda, you see. There were so many things to remind him. And I . . ."

She sounded as if she were about to cry, so I hurried to say, "Her picture's nice, Miss Judith, and I bet she would have been great in the recital." And I almost thought I heard the music echoing again. But then I've been told I have a vivid imagination.

"Yes," Miss Judith said, blinking her eyes, and not crying after all. "She was very artistic—and sensitive. Her own mother was interested in psychic things; that's why I thought we might get something from The Other Side—it's really why I joined the Psychic Society.

"Miranda would have been some kind of creative artist when she grew up, I'm sure. She used to like to help me make unusual things. She would say, 'We're good makers, aren't we?'"

"What did you make?" Tammy asked with interest.

"Well, let's see. We made strange-colored flowers —did you know a daisy will turn green if you put it in green food coloring and leave it awhile to draw the color up its stem? We made a blue rose out of a white one, too. And Queen Anne's lace— that was the prettiest of all, when we turned it all sorts of colors."

"That's neat. I'd like to try it," Tammy said. "Mother's got some food coloring, and the Queen Anne's lace is about to bloom right now."

"Be sure to cut the stem above the joint, or through the joint," Miss Judith warned, "or it'll be hard for the color to get through—and once we made a birdbath out of pretty-colored bits of broken glass and china, set like a mosaic pattern into cement. I wonder what became of that birdbath. And—oh, yes—the cement owl. I never did find the cement owl." She began to laugh a little, the kind of laugh that's nearly crying. "I haven't thought of that owl for a long time," she went on. "Miranda wanted to make an owl, she said, 'with love in its eyes.' So we did. But she hid it somewhere—and it's still hidden. That was so many years ago! I wish I could find it."

"How did she make love show in its eyes?"

"I'll tell you," Miss Judith said, standing up, so we knew it was time to go, "if you can find the owl for me. It's somewhere out in the yard. She said she discovered the right place for it, out there, a secret place. She was teasing—she said she was going to show me, as a surprise on my birthday, but—well, you girls might look for it, when you have some spare time. But be careful about snakes. Pledge cuts the grass in the front yard all right, but he hasn't weeded the edges of the yard or down there in the back for a long time. He has so many yards to take care of, I'm lucky, I guess, that he even cuts the grass in the front for me."

"Yes'm," I said. "We'll look for the owl, because I sure want to know how you made it show love in its eyes."

"Well, I'll tell you this much." Miss Judith was almost smiling again as she went to the door with us. "We used clear amber glass marbles. She called it 'the owl with the golden eyes.' "

We hunted for the owl a long time, that summer, but we never found it. Now it was another summer, and we were surprised when we were visiting Miss Judith one day to see that the picture of Miranda wasn't on the piano.

Miss Judith saw us looking puzzled and said, "I was intending to ask you girls—please don't mention Miranda while my brother and his family are here. They're coming for a visit. It's the first time since—"

"We won't," I said. "But why?"

"It is a strange request," Miss Judith agreed in her formal way. "Of course my brother's second wife knows he was married before, but he never could bring himself to tell her and their child, Sherry, about Miranda. Miranda's death hurt him so much. He blamed himself for leaving her, just as I blamed myself for . . . It hurt him so much that he has tried not to think about it ever since, tried to put it out of his mind entirely. And maybe he succeeded; maybe it's a kind of emotional block. Do you know what that is?"

"No'm," I said, but Tammy said "Yes'm," because she reads her father's psychiatry and medical books, and she told me about emotional blocks later. It's like having a blank space where you used to be able to think about something before your feelings got all mixed up.

"Anyway," Miss Judith said, "he can't bear to talk about Miranda, so it's best not to mention her. If you told Sherry, she'd be asking questions. And Dr. Alston might go to pieces if he had to explain about Miranda now, after all these years, when he's only just been able to bring himself to visit his old home again."

"Okay, Miss Judith, we understand," I said, and Tammy nodded. "How old is Sherry?"

"Why," Miss Judith said, as if she were counting it up and it surprised her, because that was the age Miranda had been, "I believe she must be—ten." Too young for us.

But not for my kid brothers. Eddie and Kirk went over to Miss Judith's right after Dr. and Mrs. William Alston and Sherry got there. The boys were invited to stay and make friends with Sherry, and they did. From then on, those two were always hanging around with Sherry.

She seemed like a nice little girl, Tammy and I agreed when we met her. But I wondered how Miss Judith—or Dr. Alston either—could bear it; she looked exactly like Miranda in the picture. The same pale, heart-shaped face and dark hair and greenish eyes and pointed chin. She was skinny and wore droopy shorts, but when you're ten you have to wear what your mother buys for you, and lots of mothers don't like to buy tight shorts—they've got a thing about pants being "comfortable."

It was several days before we really began to wonder about Sherry. Miss Judith and Mrs. Alston were sitting on the terrace under the big magnolia tree. Tammy and I were tired of playing records in my room, so we went over to talk to them. Eddie

9

and Kirk had gone to the dentist with Mama—Eddie needs braces the worst way, and Kirk's second front tooth was coming in crooked—so for once they weren't around. Miss Judith asked us to sit down and gave us each a glass of lemonade. It tasted wonderful. Tall frosted glasses of lemonade are the greatest on a hot day.

"Where's Sherry?" Tammy asked, not really caring, just being polite.

"Oh, she's around somewhere," her mother said. She called, "Sherry! Come in, please—you've got company."

"Oh, don't bother her, if she's out playing," Tammy said, in her older-girl voice, and I giggled, because after all she was only two years older than Sherry. She was trying on her adult manners.

Sherry came prancing up on a make-believe horse and hitched it elaborately at the other end of the terrace. I thought—she must be retarded or something. Even Eddie has given up riding horses that aren't there.

Miss Judith thought so too. "Isn't she a little old for that sort of thing?" she asked Sherry's mother.

"Oh, she's just reminding me that a real horse is what she wants more than anything in the world," Mrs. Alston said, laughing. "She lets us know, every chance she gets. And if I'm not careful, her father will give it to her. He gives in to her too much for her own good. He's so sensible about most things—I can't understand why he's so indulgent with Sherry."

"I wish she liked me," Miss Judith murmured. "I wish she would just come and put her arms around me or kiss me or something, the way—"

"The way what?" Mrs. Alston asked.

"The way some children do. They usually like me." She smiled at Tammy and me, and we smiled back, to let her know we understood.

"Oh, Sherry likes you," Mrs. Alston told Miss Judith. "She's just engrossed in a game she's playing, that's all. In a little while she'll be all over you—you'll see."

"That old whip—I wonder where she found that?" Miss Judith said, and she looked agitated. Sherry had a whip in her hand, the kind we used to get at carnivals, with red and black braided around the handle. But it was so old you could hardly see the color anymore. "What kind of a game is it?"

"Oh, she's a typical only child. She made up an imaginary playmate, that's all. The child psychologists call it compensation. She hasn't any brothers or sisters; so she makes up a companion to play with. That's why she doesn't need you—or me—right now."

"She has Eddie and Kirk," I said. "Eddie had an imaginary thing once. He called it Bird Dog. It was an invisible dog that could fly like a bird.

But Eddie was a lot smaller than Sherry then. And when Kirk got big enough to play with him, Eddie let Bird Dog go."

"It is a bit odd," Mrs. Alston agreed, "that she should just now be finding this imaginary child, when she has some real playmates next door. The way she talks, sometimes I think she believes this little girl is real."

Sherry looked back toward the thickest shrubbery, where a child could be hiding, and said over her shoulder as she came toward us, " 'Bye. See you tomorrow. Eddie and Kirk will be back then."

Miss Judith poured her a glass of lemonade, Tammy and I said "Hi," and Mrs. Alston said in that sickening voice grown-ups use when they try to pretend along with a child, "Where does your little friend live, honey?"

Sherry didn't have any make-believe at all in her voice. She took a sip of the lemonade, said "Hello," sort of shyly in the direction of Tammy and me, and answered matter-of-factly, "I don't know. She says she doesn't have any real home right now. Her father got a divorce from her mother. He got custody-of-the-child, but—what's custody-of-the-child, Mom?"

"It means she is supposed to live with her father, dear."

Miss Judith held out a hand to Sherry, but Sherry came over and sat on the coping next to me, instead. "Did you ever have a horse? Did Eddie?" she asked. "I want a horse of my own."

"No," I told her. "And I don't think I want one. It would be a lot of trouble to take care of."

"I'd love taking care of a horse."

Miss Judith said to Sherry, "What have you been playing, dear?"

She drew marks with the whip on the ground. "Oh, nothing. Just playing. In our Hideout."

That word did something to Miss Judith. She gasped, "Hideout!" and dropped her lemonade glass. It broke on the pretty, mossy old bricks that paved the terrace, and wasted every bit of the lemonade.

Mrs. Alston said, "What's the matter, Judith? Are you sick? You look as if you'd seen a ghost."

Right then something like a cold finger began to move up my spine, though it was a hot day.

Miss Judith said to Sherry, trying to speak calmly, "You mean, under the fig tree?" and it sounded as if she already knew.

Sherry said impatiently, "Of course. You know how the branches come down almost to the ground and the big leaves make a Hideout."

"Why do you call it that, Sherry?" Miss Judith was holding her hands together so tight the knuckles were white.

"Why, because that's what it is. Our Hideout. We haven't let Eddie and Kirk in on it yet, but we might tomorrow." She had a bland, innocent look on her face, as if she were putting somebody on, and I thought it was Miss Judith.

Poor Miss Judith didn't even try to pick up the broken glass. Tammy started to do it, but I was frozen by what was going on between Sherry and her aunt.

Miss Judith said urgently, "Sherry. Do you—does she—have a black horse tied outside the Hideout? A black horse named Nightmare?"

"Why, Aunt Judith! How did you know?" Sherry said delightedly. She went over to Miss Judith then and leaned against her shoulder, smiling up at her confidingly. The cold finger went on up my neck and made my hair prickle. "Mom," Sherry said, looking across at Mrs. Alston, "can't I please have a black horse named Nightmare for my birthday?" Her bangs were too long and she looked like a witch-child, glancing up from under them.

"What's this all about?" Mrs. Alston asked Miss Judith.

"Nothing." Miss Judith tried to pass it off, but Sherry knew. She knew something. "I'm just playing Sherry's game with her."

"Well, that's the way to win her over, all right; play games with her," Mrs. Alston said.

"Sherry," Miss Judith said, very quietly. "Sherry, what's your little friend's name?"

"I don't know, Aunt Judith. She hasn't told me her name yet."

"Where did you find that old whip, child? It's all right—you can have it—but where did you find it?"

"Oh, she knew where it was. She knows where everything is, Aunt Judith. She used to live here."

2

SOMETHING IN
MISS JUDITH'S ROOM

Miss Judith has plenty of self-control—I'll say that for her. She just closed her hands tighter. After a minute she said, "Excuse me, please," and got up and went in the house. So of course Tammy and I left.

Back in my room, we lay across the bed on our stomachs with our feet in the air, the way we usually do, and talked. "Do you think she really plays with Miranda?" I asked.

"Of course not." Tammy didn't believe in ghosts, and neither did I—but I wanted to. I'd have given anything to see a ghost.

"Then how come she knew—?"

"I don't know, but I think it might have something to do with that bunch of psychic nuts Miss Judith fools around with—the ones who have séances."

"Why do you think that?"

"I don't know," Tammy said again, thoughtfully.

"Except I saw that president or whatever he is, of the club—you know, old Mr. Carson Farrar—talking to Sherry yesterday."

"Well, he lives just across the street. He's a public relations man and I guess kids are some of the public. He talks to us sometimes, too."

"I know, but we get away from him as soon as we can."

"Right," I said. Dad told me public relations men are supposed to make everybody like some special things or companies or people, but I've never even liked Mr. Farrar himself. And it isn't because of the séances, either. It's because of last summer.

Mr. Farrar has office hours whenever he wants to; so he has time to run the Little League in this neighborhood. He kept promising Eddie that he could play in a game, and even gave him a uniform. Eddie kept going out there to practice every afternoon, and picked up the bats after the others hit the ball. The last game of all, when Eddie was so sure Mr. Farrar was going to keep his promise and let him play at least once, our whole family went out there to the field behind the clubhouse because Eddie wanted us to see him hit a home run.

But he didn't get to play at all. Mr. Farrar doesn't seem to have any feelings. He didn't even give Eddie a reason. Just said, "Too bad, Eddie. Maybe next year." He hasn't any kids of his own

—that's why he has time to belong to so many things. If he had kids maybe he'd have known enough to keep his promise, or else not make it. You just don't disappoint a little kid.

Dad told Eddie we have to be good sports about things like that, but Eddie didn't go out for Little League this summer, and I don't blame him.

Mrs. Farrar is okay, though. Even if she does go to the séances too.

"Do you suppose Mr. Farrar told Sherry about Miranda?" I asked.

"Well, Mother says the Farrars have lived here on this street since the year one; he'd have known Miranda was drowned. Sherry wouldn't have known unless somebody told her."

"But he couldn't possibly have known where Miranda hid that old whip that Sherry found. And I doubt that Miranda ever told Mr. Farrar about the Hideout or Nightmare. So it looks as if Sherry has got to be in communication with her, as they say at the séances."

"How do you know what they say?"

"I've been reading up on psychic societies."

We have lots of old books about all kinds of things—they used to belong to my grandparents. We also have a big encyclopedia in twenty volumes that a man sold Mama once, but we don't mention that very often.

"Tell me more," Tammy said admiringly.

18

"Well, nobody who has any feelings at all is ever going to remind Miranda's family about her getting drowned. It would be cruel. I don't believe even Mr. Farrar would be mean enough to fake anything like that at a séance to fool Miss Judith. So what was he doing talking to Sherry?"

"Maybe he ought to be appointed a Stranger for life," Tammy said. "One of those Strangers kids aren't supposed to talk to. We could warn her against him."

"Wouldn't do any good now. She's already met him, and knows he's a neighbor; even a dimwit like Sherry would catch on he's not really a Stranger."

"She's not actually a dimwit," Tammy objected. "She might be very bright. A genius. Sometimes they're hard to tell apart, Daddy says."

"Well, I'll ask Eddie what Mr. Farrar and Sherry were talking about."

As soon as he got back from the dentist's, Eddie showed us his new braces, and then remembered he had to feed his rabbits; so we went out in the yard with him and Kirk. The rabbits are named Brer Rabbit and Mrs. Brer, but Eddie got stubborn and wouldn't name the babies Flopsy and Mopsy and Cottontail and Peter as I suggested. He calls them One and Two and Three and Four, because he says there are going to be so many he doesn't want the names to ever run out, and numbers don't. Mark, the boy who gave the rabbits to Eddie because his mother got tired of so many of them, told Eddie to expect some baby rabbits every six weeks.

Eddie is looking forward to having a whole bunch of rabbits, but Mama isn't. And Dad makes Eddie clean out the cages every single day, or else they'll stink. The father rabbit has to be kept in a separate cage when the babies are little, or he'll kill them.

Eddie said he had no idea what Mr. Farrar was talking to Sherry about, but that Sherry had found the whip under the edge of the summer house, in a hiding place that somebody had dug out behind the foundation—which was about to cave in. Sherry fell into the hole—that was how she found the whip. "She found a bunch of other things, too," he said.

"Such as?"

"Oh, some bricks, and an old pot and spoon, and some nickels and dimes and pennies in a baking powder can—we spent those when the ice cream man came around—and some old beat-up books in a tin box, and a rubber ball that wouldn't bounce. And a lot of other old stuff."

"Did she find a cement owl with golden eyes?" I asked excitedly.

"Heck, no. What do you mean, owl with gold eyes? Owls have black eyes—I think."

"Miss Judith told us about a cement owl that got lost," Tammy explained in her talking-down-to-little-brothers voice. She hasn't got any little brothers, or she wouldn't think she could get away with that. "It had yellow glass marbles for eyes. We just wondered if Sherry had found it."

"Oh, you just wondered," Eddie mimicked. "Well, if she had, I wouldn't tell you about it." But I knew Sherry hadn't, from the way Eddie looked.

I gave Tammy the high sign and we started to leave Eddie and Kirk to the rabbits. "Don't forget their fresh water," I reminded him.

"They're my rabbits," Eddie said. "As long as they drink it, who cares if it's fresh or not? Maybe rabbits like old water best. Water doesn't wear out, since you know so much."

"I know they'll die if you don't give them fresh water every day," I said.

"Kirk's supposed to change the water anyhow," Eddie said. "I told him I'd give him Five and Six if he would."

"Kirk's too little to have all that responsibility. And besides, Five and Six aren't even born yet."

"I am not either too little," Kirk said. He was getting the water pans out as Tammy and I left.

Tammy had to go home for supper, but she said she'd call me later to see if I had dug any more out of Eddie.

I was trying to get Eddie to talk about Sherry at supper, but somehow the conversation got off the subject. It was when Eddie said, "I don't want any

21

cauliflower," and Mama said, "Why?" and Eddie said, "Because a head of cauliflower looks like somebody's brains." Well, it actually does, when you come to think about it.

Dad said, "Where did you see somebody's brains?" and Eddie said, "In Dr. Greenfield's garbage can," and Mama said, "Excuse me," and left the table in a hurry. She's going to have a baby in January, and her stomach gets upset at the least little thing.

"What were you doing in Dr. Greenfield's gar-

bage can?" Dad said, which didn't seem to me to be the most important thing to find out right then, but Eddie cleared it up when he called after Mama, "You don't have to throw up, Mama. It wasn't real brains." He told Dad, "It was a model of brains that Dr. Greenfield used for teaching students at the college. He bought a new model, so I asked him if I could have it and he said yes. I stuck it in my closet. Maybe· I better tell Mama where it is, just in case."

"That would be a good idea," Dad said. "But you aren't supposed to go scrounging around in the neighbors' garbage cans, Eddie."

"They don't mind," Eddie said. "They throw away some real good stuff sometimes."

Mama came back and said sternly, "Leave the garbage cans alone after this, Eddie!" So he didn't tell her what he found in Mr. Farrar's. It was a mouse that wasn't quite dead. Mr. Farrar lets his cat, Old Smokey, play with the mice he catches, until they're nearly dead, and sometimes he doesn't bother to put them out of their misery when he throws them in the garbage can. I just can't help not liking Mr. Farrar. Eddie put that mouse out of its misery, though, very humanely, and gave it a nice funeral.

After supper I tried to bribe Eddie to tell me more about what he and Kirk did when they were over at the Alstons' playing with Sherry, but he clammed up. I had to report "no luck" when Tammy called.

She had some real news. "Guess what?" she said. "A real live medium is coming to stay with the Farrars next week—a famous one, Daddy says. She's going to talk to the Psychic Society, and they're going to have a séance—at our house!"

"But your folks don't belong to the Society," I said. "I never thought your dad would have anything to do with ghosts."

"Silly, he's going to try to prove there's nothing to it. He says if they can show him any scientific evidence of survival after death, he wants to see it. He says he has an open mind on parapsychology and psychic phenomena, but he's extremely skeptical. Those were his very words, Lindsey."

"So how come they're going to let him show them up?"

"Well, he's sort of got Mr. Farrar in a corner, offering to have the séance at our house so there couldn't be any suggestion of fakery, he said, so the whole thing would be done in a scientific manner. This lady medium is coming next week and we'll get to see her in the flesh—Daddy says in lots of flesh. I guess she must be pretty fat."

"Hey, did your dad tell you all this, or did you—?"

"I listened," Tammy admitted. Well, there are times when you have to eavesdrop or you'll never know anything about anyone. "But he did talk about it some at supper too," she added.

"What's the medium's name?" I felt kind of excited myself, at the idea of seeing a real live medium, after what I had read about séances and mediums in those old books.

"Her name's Dame Pythia Wilks, and she's from England, where they have a lot more psychic societies than we do here. And there are witches' covens and all that kind of stuff, Daddy says. A coven is a bunch of witches that get together every now and then, like a club meeting, and sing hymns backwards and put spells on people they don't like, and such junk."

When I went over to Tammy's next day, she said we'd ask her father some more about Dame Pythia. He was at home because it was one of his research days instead of a teaching day.

Dr. Greenfield said she had a control named Kleeman who, when he was alive, was supposed to have been a World War II German soldier who learned his English in an American prisoner-of-war camp.

"What's a control?" Tammy asked.

"A medium," he said, looking at us over the top of his glasses, "can't talk directly to her audience. She's supposed to be in a trance. Her body is theoretically taken over by the spirit of the control—in this case, Kleeman—who then communicates messages from the dead in the spirit world to the people who are in the room."

I already knew that, but Tammy looked doubtful.

Dr. Greenfield went on, "If my guess is right, Dame Pythia lives on publicity. Her reputation depends on her communications being apparently true, things people who are present at a séance can recognize because of some trivial detail they think nobody knows about except the dead person."

"But fake mediums find out ahead of time everything they can," I said, "about all the people who are going to be at the séance. And the people are fooled into thinking it's their dead relatives—"

"Well, Lindsey, you seem to know a bit about fraudulent mediums," Dr. Greenfield said, smiling.

"I've been doing research," I told him. "Of course, Dame Pythia might not be. Fraudulent, I mean. She and Kleeman might be okay."

"That's what we'd like to find out, isn't it?" Dr. Greenfield said. "Because apparently she's counting on a lot of publicity here. You see, Dr. Alston is a very famous man, and if she could convince him that she can put him in touch with Miranda —well, it would mean top publicity for Dame Pythia Wilks all over the English-speaking world."

"You mean she'd actually try to—oh, poor Miss Judith!" I said, horrified. "That's the cruelest thing

I ever heard of. And it's just like Mr. Farrar. I bet it was his idea. He probably told Dame Pythia about Miranda just so she'd come here."

"Why do you say that, Lindsey?" Dr. Greenfield asked. He looked at me like a psychiatrist, which he is.

"Because Mr. Farrar does things like—well, he doesn't mind if kids suffer. Or mice."

"Hmmmm." Dr. Greenfield's eyebrows went up. "Of course, some of these psychic characters have hypnotized themselves into believing that they're doing the living a favor by putting them in touch with their dead loved ones. Maybe even that they're giving the grieving survivors some comfort.

"But I happen to have heard rumors that Mr. Farrar is helping Dame Pythia write a book about her communications from the dead. So I'm even more skeptical in this case than usual. Naturally they'd both want all the publicity they can get, to make it a best seller, and I'm curious to see how far they'll go to get it."

"I bet that Mr. Farrar was talking to Sherry just to get some background on the family for Dame Pythia to use," Tammy said.

It was a good guess, but I thought she was wrong. "He probably knows more about Miranda than Sherry does. He was here when it happened, remember?"

"But he doesn't know as much about Dr. Alston

as Sherry does," Tammy pointed out. "Maybe he doesn't even know what kind of a doctor Dr. Alston is. I don't. He's not a doctor like you, Daddy."

"No—he's a Ph.D. A Doctor of Philosophy. His specialty is physics," Dr. Greenfield said.

"Even though Sherry may not know who Miranda is, exactly," I said, "she does know about the whip and the horse named Nightmare and the Hideout. She might tell Mr. Farrar about those— if he were clever about it."

Dr. Greenfield wanted to know what I meant, so we told him about Miss Judith and Sherry's imaginary playmate. "Do you believe in ghosts, Dr. Greenfield?" I asked him.

"In a way I do," he said seriously. "The dead do come back to haunt the living—but only in their minds. In their memories. In their dreams. In their guilts. It doesn't seem likely, though, that Sherry could be troubled by Miranda, that way. She didn't have any knowledge of Miranda when she came here?"

"Miss Judith said Dr. Alston never told Mrs. Alston or Sherry about Miranda. And she asked us not to mention her, so of course we didn't."

Dr. Greenfield said thoughtfully, "I'd like to talk to that little girl."

"Are the Alstons coming to the séance?" Tammy asked.

"Not Sherry." Dr. Greenfield laughed. "Miss Alston will be here, of course, since she belongs to the group. And she will try to get Dr. Alston to come, Mr. Farrar said. Mrs. Alston will be away that weekend with her college roommate in Atlanta."

"Daddy—may we come?" Tammy begged. "Lindsey and I—we'd be quiet as—"

"No," Dr. Greenfield said definitely. "I'm sorry, Tammy—this isn't a thing for children to get mixed up in. And you two keep it quiet—don't tell your friends, understand?"

We understood, and we didn't talk to anybody about it. But we laid our plans to be there just the same, even without permission.

I was going to spend the night with Tammy, when they had the séance. Mama said I could, and Mrs. Greenfield agreed, as usual. I guess she thought it would keep Tammy up in her room and out of the way, if I were spending the night—we usually play records up there till after midnight. Little did she know. Those records drop automatically; they're long-playing ones and you can put on twelve at a time; she'd think we were playing records.

The downstairs hall closet at Tammy's house backs right up to the living room. It was built in after the house was already finished, when somebody decided they needed another closet. So it has only the one wall, a thin panel of knotty pine, between. When Tammy and I tried it out the next day while both her parents were away, there was plenty of room for us, as well as a lot of hats and raincoats.

And not only that—those knotty pine boards had knots that were easy to dig out with Dr. Greenfield's chisel, to make holes we could see through. They wouldn't be noticed at all from the living room, because that wall wasn't in direct light and the holes looked just like the other knots.

But we had to wait nearly a whole week.

To keep ourselves occupied, we concentrated on looking for the cement owl.

"Let's start in Miss Judith's summer house, because that's where Sherry found the whip," Tammy said. "Let's go ask Miss Judith if we can. Dr. Alston's gone out—his car's not in the drive. So we won't be disturbing his thinking." Mrs. Greenfield had told her never to bother Dr. Alston.

Mrs. Alston let us in, and said Sherry was out playing with Eddie and Kirk somewhere. When we said we hadn't come to see Sherry, only to ask Miss Judith something, Sherry's mother said, "She just went up to her room," and called from the foot of the stairs, "Judith! Lindsey and Tammy want to speak to you a minute."

Miss Judith called down from the hall above, "Let them come up," and we heard her opening the door to go into her room as we started upstairs.

Then we heard Miss Judith scream.

It was a dreadful scream, as if she were frightened to death.

We ran up the stairs as fast as we could.

3

THE MYSTERY OF
THE BLUE ROSE

Miss Judith was lying on the floor, white and still and crumpled.

"Is she dead?" Tammy asked, her voice quavering.

I grabbed the hand-mirror from the dressing-table and held it under her nose, and it fogged a tiny bit. "No. She's only fainted."

Mrs. Alston arrived then and dashed back to get the ammonia; when she brought it we left the first-aid to her while we looked around to see what could have frightened Miss Judith.

The room looked perfectly normal. There were flowers in the vases, and the bed was made up. Her antique furniture looked real solid. There wasn't anything supernatural about the atmosphere. No sudden cold surrounded us. No dog bristled and growled at nothing. Miss Judith doesn't even have a dog.

But I heard what sounded like a door closing.

Maybe a door that wasn't there? A door that had been boarded up, long ago?

On the other hand, it might just have been somebody else in the house, innocently closing some other room's door. Nothing abnormal about that. Only there wasn't supposed to be anyone else in the house. Could Sherry have come back, without anybody noticing?

Then I saw what had made Miss Judith faint.

The flower in the bud vase on her bedside table was a bright blue rose.

Miss Judith was sitting up now, gasping from the liberal dose of ammonia. Mrs. Alston helped her to the rocking chair. "What in the world is the matter, Judith?" she asked. "Was it an intruder— or—?"

Miss Judith wasn't about to let on about the blue rose. But we knew she was thinking that Miranda's ghost had put it there.

"I—I don't know," she said at last, in a queer voice. "Where's William? I've got to talk to him—"

"You remember. He's gone across the river to see the people he knows at that laboratory where he used to work. He might even stay overnight. Do you want a doctor? Maybe Dr. Greenfield is at home."

"No, he's at the college," Tammy said. "This is one of his teaching days."

"I don't need a doctor," Miss Judith said, and

now some of the color had come back to her face. "A doctor couldn't help me any."

I wished Mrs. Alston would go away so I could ask Miss Judith if she really thought Miranda's ghost had brought her a rose. And Mrs. Alston did go away. I wonder if I have some extraordinary power, to influence other people's actions just by wishing? No, or it would work on Eddie and Kirk too—they're the ones I do most of my wishing about.

On her way out, Mrs. Alston said, "I'm going to call and see if I can get William to come home. I'm worried about you, Judith—you've been so strange lately." And she went downstairs to the telephone in the study and shut the door so Miss Judith wouldn't hear what she told Dr. Alston.

I went and picked up the blue rose. It was a real rose, just as real as one out of the garden— except that a fine tracing of all the many tiny veins on the petals brought an odd blue color to them that no natural rose ever had. It even smelled like a rose.

Miss Judith said faintly, "It's a rose like we used to make, Miranda and I, with the food coloring—"

I stuck my finger into the vase and took it out stained blue. "There's even food coloring in the vase," I said. "Miss Judith, did you ever tell any-body—except Tammy and me—about how you and Miranda made the flowers?"

"I don't think so," Miss Judith murmured. "But," she went on thoughtfully, "William knew about it at the time. I can remember Miranda showing him some green daisies once."

"You didn't tell Sherry, for instance?" I asked Miss Judith. "Tammy and I didn't tell anybody, of course."

"Why, no, Lindsey. I never thought of—you see, Sherry isn't—well, I just can't bear the idea of any other child taking Miranda's special place, doing Miranda's special things. Sherry has her own place in my heart. But it even hurts to let her have Miranda's room. Of course I had to—there wasn't another suitable room for the child. But I couldn't have her doing the things Miranda did with me, like coloring the flowers. I'm going to teach Sherry to knit, though."

"Don't tell her anything, Miss Judith," I cautioned earnestly. "She talks to Mr. Farrar, and—well, it would be better for Dr. Greenfield's scientific investigation of that séance if Mr. Farrar didn't know a thing about Miranda."

"You girls know about the séance?" Grown-ups amaze so easy.

"Yes, but they won't let us come."

Miss Judith said, "It really would be evidential, if Dame Pythia or her control could tell me something only Miranda and I knew—"

"In the books there's one theory," I told her,

"that it's done by thought transference, instead of communicating with dead people. So try not to even think about whatever it is that only you and Miranda knew, Miss Judith. Dame Pythia might be able to do mental telepathy and read your mind, even if she can't actually get through to The Other Side. Dr. Greenfield wants scientific evidence. The whole set-up might be phony—just to get publicity, and because Dame Pythia makes a good living out of those people who believe in her. Or it just might be real. Then you'd know for sure."

"Yes," Miss Judith said.

"We came over to ask you," Tammy said, "if we could search in your summer house for the owl. We didn't look there very hard, before."

"The owl? Oh, yes," Miss Judith said, still sounding far away. "Yes, do look for it. I wish you could find it." She seemed to come back to real things. "Be careful, though—that old well curb in the summer house has probably rotted, and if you fell into the well I'd never forgive myself. So don't go near the edge of the well, you hear?"

"Yes'm," we said. At our age, we do know better than to fall in a well.

Mrs. Alston came back then, so we felt it was all right to leave Miss Judith.

The summer house's openwork lattices were all overgrown with weeds and vines, mostly honey-suckle, which was blooming. The little cream-colored trumpets smelled so sweet you could shut your eyes and think you were in Heaven. I guess in olden times when lots of Alstons lived in the house, they sat out there on summer evenings watching the fireflies, and the gardener kept the honeysuckle trimmed and the brick floor swept, and when they wanted a drink of cold water somebody drew up a bucketful from the well. But now the bricks were mossy and green and crumbling, and the vines tripped you up, and the old wicker chairs were falling apart. And Tammy and I were careful to watch out for snakes.

It was sort of sad out there, as if the ghosts of all the dead Alstons were watching us and wishing the summer house was like it used to be. I bet they played croquet, too, on the lawn in front of it, and the ladies' skirts were long and touched the grass.

We found the hidey-hole where Sherry had gotten the whip and stuff, and we dug it out further, but there wasn't anything else in that spot. Just as we were giving up we heard noises outside, and there were Sherry and Eddie and Kirk.

"What are you doing?" Eddie wanted to know.

"Yep, what are you doing?" Kirk echoed. He usually did.

"Nothing." We made it a rule to tell them as little as possible about our activities.

"I know what they're doing," Sherry said. "They're

37

looking for the owl with the golden eyes. Aren't you?" she asked Tammy. "It's not here. I already looked."

"We looked, too," Eddie said.

"Yep," Kirk said.

I asked her, "Where did you look?"

"Doncha wish you knew?" Eddie said.

"Doncha?" said Kirk.

And Sherry said, "She didn't tell me where she hid it."

"You mean the kid you said used to live here?" I was careful not to give away anything that she hadn't already revealed.

Sherry nodded. She moved over toward the edge of the well, with Eddie and Kirk behind her.

"Don't!" I said. "Don't go close to the edge. The curb is crumbly!"

"Oh, it's all right," Sherry said. "She said it was okay. She plays right by the well. You know I wouldn't let Eddie and Kirk get hurt."

I grabbed her arm and pulled her back. "You better stay away from that well. And, Eddie and Kirk, that's an order." That's what Dad always says when he really means it.

Sherry looked at me from under those long bangs of hers as if she was trying to decide whether or not to jump in the well just to spite me. Then she shrugged and skipped away, saying to the boys, "Let's go see if she's in the Hideout."

When they had gone I asked Tammy, "What do you think? Is she putting us on?"

"Hard to tell," Tammy said. "She's got the boys wrapped around her little finger, all right. They believe everything she says."

"I wonder if she was born with six fingers? I've heard if you're born with six fingers on each hand it means you can see things other people can't. Or is that if you were born with a caul? Maybe the six fingers are for witch babies. She could be a change-ling. Sometimes she looks like a witch's child instead of Mrs. Alston's."

We agreed that probably Sherry was born with a caul as well as six fingers on each hand.

"Let's ask Miss Judith," Tammy said.

"Okay, but not right now. I don't think we ought to bother Miss Judith any more today, do you? She was so shook up about the flower. Tammy, how are we going to solve the mystery of that blue rose?"

"Well, it wasn't a ghost rose, that's for sure."

"Maybe Miranda's ghost went into the kitchen and got the food coloring and fixed the rose."

"Maybe Sherry went into the kitchen and got it." Tammy was just as skeptical as Dr. Greenfield was.

"But why would Sherry want to scare Miss Judith like that?"

"She might be just a mischievous kid," Tammy

40

surmised. "Or, as Daddy would probably say, she might be trying to get some attention for herself."

"But Miss Judith didn't tell Sherry about the flowers they used to dye. If it's Miranda who's come back, now, she already knows—and she might have done it because she loves Miss Judith still, and wanted to give her a flower like they made a long time ago. Not to scare her. Or—she might have told Sherry how they did it—and maybe Sherry fixed a blue rose because she thought it would make Miss Judith love her the way she did Miranda. It's sort of sad, if Sherry's feeling left out because she found out about how they loved Miranda—and Miranda's feeling left out because Sherry's here in her place."

"Lindsey, you sound as if you really believe in Miranda's ghost. Like you think she's really around here and Sherry really sees her."

"I don't know whether I believe it or not," I admitted. "But there are lots of things even scientists haven't found out about yet. Ghosts might be one of them. Well, I don't think we're going to find the cement owl here, do you?"

"The next most likely place she might have buried it is the Hideout," Tammy said.

"But they're playing there."

"Well, tomorrow we'll ask Miss Judith if we can dig around that fig tree."

I don't especially like hard digging. "Why don't

we get Eddie and Kirk and Sherry to do the digging?" I suggested. "If we tell them we've figured out that it's buried in a certain spot, like treasure, they'd dig to China."

"You could be right. We'll let them do the hard work."

They weren't in the Hideout, though, and when we went hunting for them all over the yard we couldn't find them. Once we thought we heard them giggling behind the shrubbery beside the terrace, but nobody was there when we looked. Not even a transparent Miranda.

It was nearly dark when we came around the house and found them playing on the terrace, throwing a dirty old ball back and forth. They hadn't been there five minutes before.

"Where've you been? We were looking for you," I said.

"Nowhere." That way Sherry had of looking up slantways was catching; Eddie was doing it too, now, and of course Kirk copied everything Eddie did. "Just playing. She knew where this ball was, of course," Sherry said vaguely.

"Yep," Kirk said.

"Look, Sherry." I got in front of her to look her straight in the eyes, and the ball Kirk threw hit me in the back and rolled off into the shrubbery. "Don't you know her name yet?"

She smiled at me and ran after the ball. "Oh,

sure, I know her name now. C'mon, Eddie and Kirk!" and they ran away across the lawn. Elusive —I think that's the word for her. Or is it evasive? I'll have to look it up.

That night I cornered Eddie in the boys' room and offered him my old chemistry set if he'd tell me the name of Sherry's imaginary friend, but he wouldn't.

"I don't know what her name is," he admitted at last. "Sherry knows, though. She hasn't told us yet."

"Eddie, you don't ever see this—this kid, do you?"

"No. She's in—invisible. You know, like Bird Dog. But Sherry sees her. I used to see Bird Dog, but the rest of you couldn't. Remember?"

"I remember all right," I said sternly. "I remember you *said* you saw him. Eddie, you're too old to believe in that stuff now. Sherry's just putting you on."

"No, she's not. Sherry really does know her. Or else how could she find things her friend used to play with when she lived there?"

"Oh, Sherry just happened to find them. Anybody might happen to. They'd been lying around all those years when no children were there to be curious, that's all. If Sherry really talks to her and gets answers, how come she can't find the cement owl with the golden eyes? Why doesn't Mir—that invisible kid—tell her where she hid that?"

"I bet she will tomorrow," Eddie said hopefully, "and then if I find out her name you'll give me the chemistry set."

"Yep," Kirk said sleepily from his bunk.

"Tammy and I thought the owl might be buried under the fig tree," I said casually. "In the Hideout. You know, when Sherry's friend was playing buried treasure, all those years ago."

"It might!" Eddie said, taking the bait. "I'll tell Sherry. We'll dig all around there, tomorrow."

And we'll watch you, I thought.

"Good idea. You do have pretty good ideas sometimes, Eddie."

I gave him the chemistry set anyway; I didn't have any use for it and I needed the space in the closet. " 'Night, Eddie. 'Night, Kirk."

Then I saw what he had taken out of his pocket and put with the little bottles in the chemistry set, and I gasped.

"Eddie! Where did you get that?"

"Get what?"

"That bottle you just added to the chemistry set."

"Oh, that? I found it. Well, I—you won't tell? Mama'd kill me. Well, I got it out of the Alstons' garbage can."

It was a little square bottle that blue food coloring comes in. There was some of it still around the sides.

I grabbed it. "I'll bring it back," I promised. "I've got to show it to Miss Judith—" and I ran out before he could object.

I slipped out the back door because Mama might have thought it was too late to go visiting, and hurried over to the Alstons'. They were sitting on the front porch. Dr. Alston wasn't back yet, I guessed, because his car wasn't in the drive, and Sherry was just starting to go to bed.

I probably should have broken the news more gently, but I was so excited I just burst out, "Look, Miss Judith, what Eddie found in your garbage can!" and I held out the blue bottle. "Somebody," I panted, "knew about the food coloring and all—"

The porch light was on, and she could see what it was. It shook her up, all right. She put her hand up to her heart, and I for one wished Dr. Alston would hurry up and come back. She needed somebody to talk to, and she couldn't tell Mrs. Alston what was the matter.

Sherry laughed, and it was a thin silvery sound. She whirled around and around in her nightgown, and I thought about elves and fairies and changelings. "Oh, did you find it?" she asked Miss Judith. "Did you find—the blue rose?"

"Child—Sherry—did you—?"

"I made it for you," she said, and her voice was innocent.

"You made it?"

"She told me how."

I shivered. So did Miss Judith—or she was trembling, anyhow.

Sherry whirled over and kissed her mother, then went and kissed Miss Judith's cheek. " 'Night, Mom, 'Night, Aunt Judith."

Miss Judith said in a queer half-choked voice, "She? Who? *Who*, Sherry?"

Mrs. Alston said indulgently, "Don't you know your little friend's name yet, Sherry?"

Sherry was at the screen door now, ready to go upstairs. She was holding the screen half open, letting all the candleflies get inside, but Miss Judith didn't tell her to shut the door. She just held her breath and waited for Sherry to answer.

"Sure," Sherry said at last, impishly. "Of course I know her name."

"What is it, then?" Mrs. Alston didn't really care; she was just making conversation. But Miss Judith leaned forward, clasping her hands together as if she were saying grace, only tighter.

There was a long pause, and then Sherry said directly to Miss Judith, "Her name's Miranda, Aunt Judith. *You* know."

"That's a pretty name," Mrs. Alston said.

Miss Judith said faintly, "Did you—ever—hear it before, Sherry?"

Maybe she was thinking some of us who knew about Miranda had let it slip, but Sherry smiled dreamily, her eyes half closed. "No. I don't think I ever heard it before. Aunt Judith—" Her voice trailed off sleepily, "don't you remember her—Miranda?"

"No! No!" Miss Judith said hysterically. "Of course—it's impossible—you made her up—" That Sherry was enough to give anybody hysterics, especially her relatives.

The screen door slammed, and Sherry and the candleflies were inside. But I didn't hear her running up the stairs. She slipped away silently, like a ghost.

Dr. Alston's car turned in the drive. "There's her father now," Mrs. Alston said. "He can go and tuck her in, Judith. Maybe he can calm down that wild imagination of hers. Let's go to bed, too. You can talk to William in the morning."

Miss Judith had recovered that special dignity of hers. "Yes," she said. "Goodnight, Olivia. Goodnight, Lindsey. Thank you for bringing me the little bottle."

"Eddie wants it for his chemistry set," I said. "May I have it for him?"

"Of course." Miss Judith even smiled a little.

"Goodnight," I said to them both.

Mrs. Alston murmured, "Miranda! What a name to make up."

I saw Miss Judith give a start, and in a minute I realized that she heard something. Something besides the name Miranda. Because I heard it too. I know I did.

It was the hesitant, tinkly sound of soft, single piano notes, very faint and faraway.

Miss Judith almost ran into the house, and the screen slammed behind her. She'll catch whoever's at the piano, I thought. Mrs. Alston looked after her, shaking her head worriedly.

"Didn't you hear anything, Mrs. Alston?" I said.

"Only some music, maybe a radio playing, Lindsey. Probably in Dr. Alston's car, you know, out on the drive."

A radio. Well—possibly.

Or it could have been Sherry fingering that piano, I told myself as I went back home. I had heard she used to study music. But I bet if it was Sherry, she had dashed up the back stairs and was in bed with her eyes shut by the time Miss Judith got to the piano.

I still felt shivery, though. A radio—why would a pianist play that particular tune—and with one finger?

But then, how would Sherry know Miranda used to play *The Dance of the Fireflies*?

4

A LONESOME
LITTLE GHOST

Tammy and I might not have overheard Miss Judith and Dr. Alston talking next day, if we hadn't happened to find out where Sherry and the boys had been hiding while we were looking for them, the afternoon before. It was a place Sherry had heard about from Miranda, Eddie told me later. After Sherry shocked Miss Judith with the name, she didn't mind the boys knowing it, too.

I met Tammy at the back hedge as usual, because we had planned to search every inch of the Alstons' yard for the cement owl, that morning. The kids were already digging around the fig tree on the other side of the house, and we meant to keep an eye on them, too.

Tammy said mysteriously, "I think I know where they were yesterday afternoon, Lin. It's a great hiding place, too."

"And just wait till I tell you about last night!" I said.

"What happened?"

We sat down on Miss Judith's marble garden bench and I told Tammy about the blue coloring bottle and Sherry making the rose, and telling Miranda's name, and then the eerie music. Tammy said, "I bet it was just the radio, though. That's what they call coincidence, you know."

"It was no coincidence, Tam. It was no radio. Why, there was even a wrong note, like when a kid makes a mistake in practicing, and goes back and strikes the right one. And besides, it gave me goosebumps. And I'm getting them again, just talking about it."

"Maybe you ought to have a physical."

"Don't you ever have goosebumps when you think about Miranda?"

"No. Not really. I kind of pretend to myself that I think she's a ghost, sometimes, because it would be so great if it were really true about ghosts. But no, I guess I'm a—whatever it is Daddy is."

"Skeptic. Well, I'm halfway between," I said honestly. "Now tell me where they were hiding, and how you found out."

"Come on, I'll show you. First let's look on the other side, and be sure they're still digging."

They were. The big leaves of the fig tree made a good screen, but we could see activity behind them. Tammy said, "They won't be able to see us; the house is between. Come on."

She led the way around to the other side of Miss Judith's house. "You don't see it?"

"No. Nothing but lawn and trees and a lot of overgrown shrubbery over toward our place, and her day lilies are beginning to bloom."

"And her magnolias," Tammy said significantly. There was an enormous old magnolia tree shading the terrace close to the house, some of the limbs touching it. The leaves were long and thick and green, and a few of the big white cup-shaped flowers showed up among them.

"I get it!" I said. "You mean, they were up in the tree hidden behind the leaves."

"Right," Tammy said. "I saw Sherry coming down from it earlier this morning. I don't think she saw me, though. I was sort of behind the hedge. It was before Eddie and Kirk came over."

"It looks easy to climb—it would have to be, for Kirk to get up there. The limbs are almost like a ladder on both sides. Let's go up."

I went first, and we both had reached the first-floor level of Miss Judith's house—it's high off the ground with a basement underneath, where the kitchen used to be when there were lots of servants —when we heard her voice. But she wasn't talking to us.

I put my finger on my lips, and Tammy nodded. We both held our breaths and kept very still, and I'm ashamed to say we listened. Miss Judith was

talking to Sherry's father in the study that used to be Miss Judith's father's. He was a minister and needed a study. I guess it was Dr. Alston's study, too, when he lived there.

The first thing I heard was Miss Judith saying, "I put away all the photos. And nobody has told her. But she knows. William, she knows about Miranda!"

Dr. Alston's voice said, "And Olivia? Does Olivia know?"

"Not yet. She thinks Miranda is a playmate that Sherry imagines. And I don't know—I can't be sure whether Sherry knows just who Miranda is— was. But, William, she knows things you and I never told her—how to color the flowers—and she found the whip you bought Miranda at the carnival that time—and she knows about Nightmare and the Hideout under the fig tree."

Dr. Alston's voice was a little husky. "There must be an explanation. Somebody must have told her. I should have told her, and Olivia, a long time ago. But at first I couldn't. Then it seemed too late. They wouldn't understand. It's hardly a rational thing, this crazy grief I still feel. Especially here, where Miranda was."

"Nobody knew," Miss Judith's voice said, "about Nightmare and the Hideout. Except Miranda. And you and I."

I could tell Miss Judith was crying, even before

Dr. Alston said, "Don't cry, Judith. Here, take my handkerchief—"

After a pause he said, "You gave her Miranda's room. Was there anything there? Anything that might have told Sherry—?"

"Miranda herself might have been there—"

I had the cold shivers, hearing that, even though the summer sun was shining hot outside the dim green place where we hid in the leaves. The magnolia flowers smelled sweet, but it was kind of decayed-sweet. And when I glanced at Tammy, she wasn't looking so awfully skeptical just then, either. When a squirrel scurried down from the top of the tree and passed us, we nearly fell off the limb.

Dr. Alston said slowly, sadly, "In that room? You know Miranda is—not anywhere, Judith. Not there. Not here. Not anywhere."

"William, we don't know. Suppose—just suppose it's true that spirits can come back. Maybe she wasn't disturbed until Sherry seemed to have taken her place here. Maybe Miranda thinks we've forgotten her. And maybe she wants us reminded that she was our little girl, too. I'll never forgive myself —when Sherry said Miranda's name and asked if I remembered her, I said no! Because you hadn't told Olivia, I thought it'd be best for her to think Sherry made her up. I denied Miranda, William.

I denied she'd ever existed. I shouldn't have done that. She has to haunt me, now."

"Judith, that Psychic Society isn't good for you. There's no need for you to feel so guilty about a white lie like that. I hope you'll drop out of the society and join a garden club or something wholesome."

"William, I've been wanting to ask you about the society. Mr. Farrar invited Dame Pythia Wilks to come here, and she accepted. She's the famous trance medium from England, you know. The séance will be held at Dr. Greenfield's house, because he wants it to be as scientific as possible, with no chance of fraud. He wants to investigate psychic phenomena and try to prove it's trickery. But he might get convinced. Anyway, I want you to come with me to that séance. It's next weekend, when Olivia will be gone to visit her friend in Atlanta. Maybe Dame Pythia will get through to Miranda for us."

"Why would a famous trance medium come here? There can't be much money in it for her," Dr. Alston said.

"She's giving a lecture in Atlanta, and Mr. Farrar persuaded her somehow to come over here for one night. It's not too far, and I'm sure the Society will put up an honorarium for her. A good many of the officers are very well off, you know. Besides being president of our branch, Mr. Farrar belongs to the National Psychic Society too, and met Dame Pythia in New York at their convention last year. You'll go with me to the séance, won't you, William? And if—if Miranda's there, we won't deny her again."

Dr. Alston said, "Well, I'll tell you what, Judith. I'll make a deal with you. I'll go—if you'll agree to give up the Psychic Society. I mean, when something happens there to convince me that it's a fraud, then you'll quit it completely."

"All right," Miss Judith agreed. "That's fair enough, William. If there's nothing evidential enough to prove Miranda's with us, then I'll stop having anything at all to do with the Society. Because if anything is ever going to come through from Miranda, this would surely be the time."

"Well, don't think about it until then," Dr. Alston said. "Please, Judith. I'm worried about you. I'm certain Miranda's at rest, not playing with Sherry, and I want you to be certain too."

"Do you suppose Sherry could have overheard us mention Miranda?" Miss Judith asked. You know, we did talk about her the second day after you came, when Olivia was upstairs and we were here in the study. If Sherry was where she could hear us, and realized who Miranda was—"

Tammy and I nodded at each other. We knew where Sherry was, all right, when she overheard them. But it left lots of things still unexplained.

56

"That might be it." Dr. Alston sounded relieved. "She might have subconsciously remembered the name, and used it for her imaginary friend."

"But we didn't mention any details that Sherry somehow knows. Only her name."

"Now stop worrying about it, Judith. You've agreed to let the whole thing rest on how that séance turns out. Make us some coffee, will you? You always made the best coffee. I wish you'd teach Olivia how."

As their voices faded away Tammy and I got down from the tree in a hurry, before anybody could see us.

"Poor Miss Judith," Tammy said as we went to see how the digging was coming along. "How disappointed she's going to be after that séance."

"I wonder," I said. "There are two other possibilities, Tam. One is, that something 'evidential' will happen—it means, I guess, evidence that points to the truth. The other is, that Mr. Farrar will *make* some evidence show up. And that would be worse for Miss Judith than if nothing at all happened. He might be able to do it if he pumped Sherry enough. Or if he remembers enough about Miranda."

"Did it ever occur to you, Lin," Tammy said, "that this may be a case of dual personality? Sherry and Miranda might be the same. I don't mean the real Miranda; I mean the one Sherry made up. Or pretends about. Or sees. Or whatever. Sometimes the good and bad sides of a person split—and Sherry does have a way of blaming Miranda for things like going near that old well. Sometimes a little kid will make up an imaginary playmate who does all the bad things that he himself really does. Maybe Sherry is setting up Miranda to take the blame for anything she doesn't want to be blamed for."

"She's too old for that."

"No—dual personalities can be in grown-ups, too. Don't you remember that movie, *The Three Faces of Eve,* that we saw on TV? That was a case of triple personality."

"Maybe, Tam—but I still think Sherry's found out somehow about who the real Miranda was, and is simply jealous because Miranda was first and she thinks they loved her more. So she's trying everything she can, good and bad, to get their attention. Seeing Miranda is one way to do it."

Tammy said, "I don't see what Sherry's got to be jealous about. She's alive, she's here, and from what I hear she gets everything she wants from her father. How can she think he doesn't love her as much?"

"She can tell. He's just giving her things to make up for not giving them to Miranda. I bet she senses that everything her father does for her somehow goes back to his feeling about Miranda. It would make anybody feel bad."

We had come to the Hideout now, and Tammy said, "Found it yet?"

Sherry looked up slantways from under her bangs and admitted, "No. But we will!"

Tammy and I would have liked to find the owl with the golden eyes before Miss Judith's birthday, which we had discovered was the following week. We wanted to show her where it was hidden, as a birthday surprise, the way Miranda had planned. She hadn't had time to do it; maybe that was why her spirit couldn't rest. Unfinished business. If we could do this for Miranda, maybe she could be at peace, and the haunting would be finished. That's the way I figured it, anyhow. Tammy just thought it would be fun to find it and surprise Miss Judith, and find out how they had put love in its eyes.

"C'mon," Sherry said to Eddie and Kirk, and they dropped their tools and followed her as if they'd been hypnotized. She really had them with her, all right.

"It's kind of funny," Tammy said, as we looked around where they'd been digging, "that Sherry doesn't simply say Miranda told her where the owl is, and bring it out."

"Maybe Miranda doesn't want Sherry to be the one to find the owl. It would spoil her birthday surprise for Miss Judith. Maybe she's jealous of Sherry."

"There you go again. Talking like that ghost is real, Lin."

"She's real as long as somebody thinks she is. It gives me a queer feeling when I think about having so much power in my mind. I can keep Miranda alive—I, Lindsey—if I find the owl I can *be* Miranda for a minute and give Miss Judith her birthday surprise, and then lay Miranda's spirit to rest."

"Now you're giving me the shivers," Tammy complained. "There's nothing here, anyhow. They dug pretty well everywhere, and pretty deep."

"Not quite down to China, but deep enough," I conceded. "Well, where do we look next?"

"She told Miss Judith it was somewhere in the yard," Tammy said thoughtfully. "There's a kind of dense thicket in that back corner where the hedge goes over into your yard. Pledge never gets in there to cut grass or trim it or anything. But when Miranda lived here it wasn't like that. She could have gotten in there easy, and put the cement owl in a little niche or something in that fieldstone wall that goes across the back behind the hedge."

"That's a good place." I gave Tammy credit. It was just the sort of place Miranda might have chosen. She might even have taken one of the loose rocks out of the wall and made the niche. "Let's look at every inch of that wall. She could have made a niche anyplace along it, and things could have grown up in front of it."

"Don't let the kids see what we're doing," Tammy said.

But before we could hack a way through the briars with Pledge's scythe that we got out of Miss Judith's woodhouse, there was Sherry, closely backed up by Eddie and Kirk. "We found a snake in there yesterday," she said innocently.

"Yep," Kirk said.

"Aw, it was probably just an earthworm," Tammy said. "They look like snakes sometimes, the big ones do."

"No. It was a snake, a poisonous snake. Miranda said so. But she said for us to pick it up if we wanted to. She said we shouldn't be afraid of snakes."

"You didn't pick it up, though?"

"No," Sherry said. "I would've except I don't like snakes that much. Eddie tried to pick it up but it got away."

"Eddie!" I was acting like a big sister again. "Don't you ever touch anything that wiggles, you hear me? Or Kirk either. It could kill you! You'd die in horrible agony if it ever happened to be a poisonous snake instead of a worm!"

"It's okay—" Sherry danced away, singing the words, with Kirk and Eddie playing follow-the-leader behind her. "Miranda likes snakes, and worms too—" They were all singing it at the tops of their voices as they skipped out of sight around the corner of the house.

Something about that whole thing was worrying me, and finally I realized what it was. I turned to Tammy. I don't know what I'd do without Tammy to talk things over with. We hardly ever agree about anything, but we sure do get our ideas lined up better when we have to defend them against each other's objections. "Tammy. You know what all this sounds like? It sounds like Miranda is trying to get those kids into danger. Remember she said it was all right for them to go near the well? And now she wants them to pick up snakes."

"Nobody proved it was Miranda. It's Sherry who said Miranda said that." Tammy always put her finger on the right objection. "Proves my theory about Sherry wanting somebody to blame for anything wrong she does."

"Sherry wouldn't want to get herself or the kids in real danger. But Miranda—"

"Miranda wasn't a wicked child," Tammy reminded me. "She was just a poor little kid who didn't have her mother to go to—and she fell in the pond when the edge caved in at the deep part, and she couldn't swim. She wasn't mean or anything."

"Eddie and Kirk can't swim either. I wonder if

Sherry can?" I glanced over toward the Hideout, and almost thought I could see something move behind the leaves—some transparent shadow of an elfish child, a lonely child whose mother wasn't around, who had only her aunt. Poor little Miranda. "Well, listen, Tammy, suppose she isn't wicked or mean, but just lonesome. A lonesome little ghost whose father won't acknowledge that he once had a little girl named Miranda? Maybe she doesn't want to hurt them, but only to get them over on the other side. She might want playmates she could keep forever—wherever it is she has to spend forever—and they have to die to be like her—"

"Do shut up, Lindsey!" Tammy looked a little bit scared. "You're giving me goose pimples again. And I don't even believe in all that. Sherry's just trying to see how far she can go toward danger without actually doing anything really dangerous. She wouldn't let the kids get hurt. She's just teasing you because you let her see that it shakes you up. Don't pay any attention to her and she'll drop it."

"Just the same, I'm going to order Eddie and Kirk not to go near that pond, with or without Sherry. I think they're in danger. From one or the other—Sherry or Miranda."

"It's lunch time," Tammy said, shrugging. "You can tell them when you go to lunch. We'll finish examining the wall this afternoon. I do think it's a great place to look. That niche idea is the best one we've had yet."

We each went home to eat. I cornered Eddie and Kirk in the bathroom—Mama told me to see that they washed their hands because they had been playing with earthworms, though they assured her it was snakes. "You two stay away from the pond," I said, "and that's an order!"

"Don't worry, we aren't going near that old pond," Eddie said. "Not never."

"Why, that's fine, but how come you decided that?"

"Because," Eddie said.

"Yep, because," Kirk said. His hands were filthy, and I had to help him scrub them. Eddie was wiping his on the towel, but some dirt still showed besides what he left there.

"Because Miranda's afraid of the pond, that's why. It's the only thing she's afraid of, Sherry says."

5

DANGER AT
MIDNIGHT

Well, it was more likely, Tammy and I decided, that Sherry had been told to stay away from that pond. I would've told her to, if I'd been her parents or her aunt. But of course she wouldn't want Eddie and Kirk to know she couldn't do everything around there that she wanted to. That would've spoiled her image, for them.

Tammy and I checked every inch of the wall, that afternoon, and found several places, where stones were missing, that could once have been niches for an owl with golden eyes. But there was no owl. It was a real disappointment.

Eddie and Kirk and Sherry stuck around for awhile, watching us hack away the briars and even helping a little. When we got to the corner of the lot, where the side street leads over to the shopping centre, we saw Mr. Carson Farrar.

Of course, he had to stop and ask what we were doing, being nosey like he is, and of course Kirk had to tell him, being too little to know that the less you say to Mr. Carson Farrar the better. "Lookin' for the cement owl with golden eyes that M'randa hid."

I told Kirk Mama wanted him and Eddie, but it was no use. They spilled all the details they knew, and even something we didn't know, that Miranda must have told them through Sherry. They said that Miss Judith and Miranda made the owl by putting wet cement in a plastic bag and shaping it like an owl, then made finger holes for the eyes and drew lines for the wings and claws through the plastic into the wet cement; they let it dry in the plastic, and then peeled the plastic off after it was dry. If Miranda could tell Sherry all that, it really was funny that she wouldn't tell her where it was hidden. But then, we figured, Sherry might know where it was and just wasn't saying. You can't tell about that kid.

Mr. Farrar said he hoped we'd find the cement owl, but of course he didn't really hope so.

Eddie said, "Maybe you could make one in your workshop, Mr. Farrar."

"Yep," Kirk said.

"What would I want to make a thing like that for?" Mr. Farrar shook his head, and went on home. I was glad to see him go, because we still had a bit more of the wall to check.

But we didn't find the cement owl. It was a

whole afternoon wasted. Well, we hadn't much else to do, anyway.

I don't know whether to blame Sherry or not for what happened that night. I do know, though, that it wouldn't have happened—at least not that night—if Mrs. Brer hadn't decided to have her babies, and Eddie and Kirk hadn't sneaked out in the middle of the night to help deliver them.

When I got up to get a drink of water and saw their closed door, I knew right away that was where they were. Usually they leave their door, as well as all the other doors they go through, wide open. There had to be a reason for that closed door— they weren't in their room, and didn't want anybody to know it.

Naturally, I looked in. I remembered that at supper Eddie had said Mrs. Brer was acting funny, and he looked speculatively at Mama, and Dad said, "That's enough, Eddie." Because a gentleman doesn't think about a pregnant lady and a pregnant rabbit in the same category like that. Even if they are both mammals.

I didn't know how long Eddie and Kirk had been gone, or how long it takes a rabbit to have babies, but I thought I ought to go look, and get them back to bed before they got into trouble for being out. And I was curious, too, about Mrs. Brer and exactly how rabbits have babies.

My clock said ten minutes to midnight. I slipped into my shorts and shirt, and hurried down to the back yard. I looked for Dad's flashlight, on the shelf in the pantry, but it was gone. So I knew Kirk and Eddie had it. I went back upstairs for my own flashlight. It was a dark night, and I wished Tammy had been spending the night with me, so I'd have somebody along when I went out there. I felt as if Miranda might be over there in Miss Judith's yard in the dark, sitting on that phantom horse Nightmare, watching me across the hedge. It was a hot night, but I shivered.

Well, Eddie and Kirk weren't at the cage. They had been there, though—Eddie had had enough sense to move Brer into the other cage. The first family of young was huddled in the corner of Mrs. Brer's cage. She was hiding way back in the straw, and there were funny little almost-not noises.

I flashed the light into the cage, but I couldn't see much; Mrs. Brer had dug deep into the straw. I wondered about the baby rabbits; I thought Five and Six at least might have come by now, if not Seven and Eight. It was strange that Kirk wasn't right there, dying to see his two.

Where could the kids be? I felt danger all over me, in every goosebump.

Everything was too still—like before a thunderstorm—hot and still and dark. The way it is just before the wind picks up and starts blowing the trees around and some big drops come down and the clouds hit together and the lightning looks like a bare white tree branch with twigs forking out.

I stood there by the cage and held my breath, and there wasn't a sound anywhere, except Mrs. Brer scuffling in the straw. I called softly, "Eddie— Kirk—" but I didn't want to wake Mama and Dad and get the boys in trouble. I flashed the light around, but couldn't see any sign of them. They must have gone over to Alstons' yard, I thought— that little witch Sherry was probably flitting around on her broom and had enticed them over there at midnight to do something mysterious. And they'd go anywhere Sherry said. They aren't scared of the dark, either.

But I was, a little, at this point. Did I dare go over there? It shouldn't have been any different than any other night, and I'd been out at night lots of times. But somehow it felt different. Maybe because it was late. And still. There weren't even any cars going past on the street; it would have been comforting to see a couple of headlights come around the corner. Anyhow, I felt more alone than I'd ever felt in my life.

But just because I was scared, I had to do it. To show myself that being scared is normal and you get over it if you're brave enough to face up to it. Only, I didn't quite know what I was scared of. But I thought it might be Miranda's ghost.

I went cautiously across our yard, and the grass felt damp and dewy, and I realized I hadn't put on any shoes. My feet didn't make any noise on the grass, but when I went through the hole in the hedge, the dead bits crackled loud as pistol shots.

There in front of me was the Hideout.

The big fig leaves drooped around it, and when I flashed my light they looked flat and black-green. Did I dare look inside that cave of darkness? Maybe it was only Eddie and Kirk and Sherry hiding in there, waiting to jump out at me. But suppose it was Miranda in there—holding a cement owl with golden eyes? Not the real one—a ghost owl with spooky eyes—an owl you could see through?

Then I thought—and it was a curiously comforting thought—about the fact that the real owl had love in its eyes. Sherry didn't seem to know about that. And Miranda couldn't be so bad, if she wanted it to have love in its eyes.

So I pushed the drooping branches aside, and slipped into the Hideout. The leaves fell back behind me with a soft rustle, like a heavy curtain. I noticed in panic that my flashlight was getting dimmer—the batteries were old. This was the worst possible time for them to give out. In the thin light before the batteries went dead I could see that nobody was in the Hideout but me.

Unless—was that Miranda behind the shadow of the tree's big trunk? I almost thought I could see

70

a transparent movement, a wisp of dark hair, and a white something that would be a pixie face. But I knew it was my imagination.

Then my light went out and I stood in the dark, rooted to the ground with plain terror.

I swallowed hard, and said out loud, "Love in its eyes—" as if that could make a difference. It was the first thing that came into my head, and I latched onto it. And suddenly I felt less scared. I wasn't exactly relaxed, but at least I wasn't rigid.

On impulse, I spoke to Miranda, just as if she were there. "Miranda—what is it you want?"

71

There wasn't a sound. Which doesn't prove she wasn't there.

Well, anyhow, I knew that Eddie and Kirk weren't. I parted the branches again and left the Hideout and walked across Miss Judith's yard, just as if I felt as brave as I wished I did.

Across the street, I could see lights at the Farrars'. Probably they were having a secret meeting of the Psychic Society's inner sanctum, to organize things for the séance. Usually, according to the books about proceedings of such societies, they had somebody to tape-record everything the medium communicated, so they could study it later and check out everything the control said. Nearly always, if they tried hard enough afterwards, somebody could remember a dead friend or relative whose initial was J or whatever, and who had something about automobiles in his past, and was taking medicine when he died, and vague things like that, which "checked."

Maybe the officers of the Psychic Society were at the Farrars' deciding how many of the members they'd let come to this very private séance. Dr. Greenfield had told Tammy that only about ten of them were going to know about it at all. And if it weren't kept a secret from the others, they'd be mad because they weren't invited. A Dame Pythia Wilks séance was the greatest thing that could ever happen in a Psychic Society, and the left-out members might tar and feather Mr. Farrar if it leaked out, Dr. Greenfield said. And that might be a real good idea, Tammy and I had agreed privately. We had never seen anybody tarred and feathered, but we couldn't think of a better one to start with than Mr. Farrar.

While I was standing there looking at the lights in the Farrars' house, I forgot to be so frightened. From this angle the Alstons' house seemed to be all dark, though I knew if Miss Judith happened to be over at the Farrars' the night-light would be on in her front hall. I thought I'd see if it was.

I slipped around to the front, and sure enough, there was a dim light showing through the glass in the door. I circled to the other side of the house, then, wondering if Eddie and Kirk were up in Sherry's room with her. They could have gotten into her window by climbing that magnolia tree, I thought when I stood under it, because her room was right over the study, and one of the big limbs of the tree actually touched the roof, which sloped only a little under Sherry's window. It was a house that had different levels of roofs, and her window was on the second floor. There was an attic window even higher up, above hers.

Sherry's room (she had taken us up there once) was real pretty, the way Miss Judith had fixed it up for Miranda. Only Sherry thought it was for her. Or did she? Sometimes I felt sure all Sherry's tricks were just sort of desperate bids for Miss

Judith's love—and then again I was doubtful. But
—that blue rose. Could either of them think Miss
Judith would *like* it?

There I was, thinking about Miranda again, and
the eerie feeling came back. Miranda had climbed
this very same magnolia tree—maybe she had used
it to get in and out of her window, if she wanted to
slip out and not let them know she was gone.

The old magnolia tree must have been pretty
big even when Miranda lived in that room up
there. Some of its branches were higher than the
rooftop now—they'd reached beyond her window,
even then.

Kirk and Eddie could have climbed up there—
only it would have been silly to do that, when
Sherry could've just come down and let them in the
door. And since there wasn't any light in Sherry's
room, I concluded they must be somewhere else.

Then a thought struck me that turned me cold.
The pond! What if they had gone down to the
pond? I had only Eddie's word for it that Miranda
didn't want them to—and Sherry might decide to
take them down there anyway. I had told Dad he
should teach Eddie and Kirk to swim, and he
laughed and said, "Why not you, too?" I told him
it wasn't so necessary for me. Now I saw that it
could be necessary. If one of them was drowning,
I couldn't save him.

I ran, and it seemed like a mile to the edge of

the pond, though it was just past the summer house. But down there at the end of the yard the dark was thick and different—I guess it was the fog that formed over the water. Not a bit of light came from anywhere, so I could barely see the pond. There was a wet, dank smell, and suddenly I thought about all of Edgar Allan Poe's tarns. That pond would have made a great tarn. Without any trouble at all, I could imagine dripping, decaying skeletons rising out of it. I was still clutching the useless flashlight; it seemed better to have something to hold onto even if it was only that.

Was that a movement of some kind, over there where the edge of the pond had once caved in?

Was it—Miranda?

Even though she was afraid of the pond, as Eddie said, it might be that ghosts *had* to return and haunt the place where they died, whether they wanted to or not.

There was something moving, down there in the dark.

Maybe it's only a water moccasin, I thought. That shows you how scared I was, thinking hopefully of a water moccasin instead of a ghost.

I whispered, "Eddie? Kirk? Are you there? Answer me!" and then wondered why I was whispering. I said it out loud, and my voice sounded so strange —the croak of it frightened me as much as if it had been somebody else's weird voice. "Eddie! Kirk!"

If they had been there, they had already drowned, I thought, shuddering. All three of them might be floating out there with weeds in their hair like Ophelia, and couldn't answer.

And then the storm broke. All of a sudden there were huge drops of rain pelting me, and lightning coming and going made the pond show up and then disappear, a great shining black flat blob; and then nothing but dark space again. But I saw with great thankfulness that there were no bodies floating on it with weeds in their hair.

Then I heard the terrified screams.

6

THE SECRET
PLACE

The frightened, wild screaming seemed to come from somewhere behind me, from the Alston house. I whirled around, and saw a light come on outside their back door, and Dr. Alston rushing out, tying a robe on over his pajamas. He had heard it too. It wasn't just my imagination.

I ran toward him, and we met nearly in front of the summer house. Just about that time there was another yell from inside the summer house. I recognized Eddie's voice.

"It's Eddie," I panted, and Dr. Alston ran inside with me behind him. Eddie's flashlight pointed toward the old well. He was crying, "Kirk's in there! Kirk fell in!"

Sherry was leaning over the well curb, and for a moment I had a mean thought—is she pushing him down or trying to get him out? But Dr. Alston grabbed her and pushed her back and leaned over, himself. We could hear Kirk hollering now too.

Dr. Alston said, "Hand me that flashlight." Eddie did.

Dr. Alston flashed the light down into the well, holding on with his other hand to the strongest edge he could find. "Hang onto the chain, Kirk!" he commanded. "Don't let go. I'll get you out. Just hold on!"

Kirk was scared to death. He was sobbing out loud, but I was proud of him—he caught his breath and said, "Yes, sir," before he started screaming again.

"The rest of you stay way back from the well!" Dr. Alston said sternly, and I thought maybe Sherry was in for it, this time. But Dr. Alston was too busy rescuing Kirk to even wonder why we were all out there.

The well had water in it; we could hear Kirk splashing whenever he had to stop crying to breathe. But we didn't know whether it was deep enough to drown him. I thought of water moccasins and shivered. There were probably all sorts of terrible things down there. Even skeletons.

Dr. Alston was testing the edge, trying to find a firm place to lean while he reached for Kirk. The chain that had held the well bucket looked so rusty I was afraid it would break if he tried to pull Kirk up by it. He evidently thought so too, because he told me, "Lindsey, will you go to the garage and

the woodshed and see if there's some strong rope there?"

"Yes, sir!" I said. "But my flashlight batteries are dead. How can I find the rope in the dark?"

"I'm afraid I'll need the flashlight here, in case the chain should break before you get back," Dr. Alston said. "Maybe the light from the back door will help some. Wait a minute—take these matches —and be careful with them. Hurry now!"

I took the matches and ran for the garage. I couldn't see any rope there. But in the woodshed there was a rope coiled up and hanging on a nail. It looked pretty old, but it was thick. It looked long enough, too—though of course I had no idea how deep the old well was. I was so nervous I dropped a match and had to stop to be sure the flame was out. I lit another, grabbed the rope off the nail, and started back toward the summer house. The rain had stopped.

Just then Mrs. Alston came out of the back door in her nightgown, saying, "What's going on? William! Sherry's not in her room!" And Miss Judith came around the corner of the house—probably from the Farrars' where the meeting had broken up—saying, "What's the matter?"

I hollered to them, "Kirk's in the old well!" and rushed on with the rope.

Dr. Alston kept saying, "Hang on, boy!" while he tied the rope to a tree just outside the summer house and knotted a loop in the other end of it that would slip tight when pulled. He lowered it to Kirk. "Can you hang on with one hand and get the rope over your shoulders and under your arms?"

"No, sir," Kirk sobbed. "I'll fall and drown!" He was so scared, poor kid. So was I, but I said, "Dr. Alston, how about tying me to the end of the rope and letting me down there so I can tie the rope on Kirk? Or maybe he can just hold onto my neck while you pull us both up—"

Dr. Alston said, "You're a brave girl, Lindsey. But I think I'd better tie the rope around myself and go down there after him. I believe I can climb back out by pulling myself up with it, and using the rocks at the sides of the well to put my feet on." He saw Mrs. Alston and Miss Judith then, and said, "Get my flashlight from the car, please, Olivia, and if you have one, Judith, do get it, too. I'll need more light." He had drawn the loop up and was tying it around his waist.

"Is there time to call somebody to help?" Miss Judith said.

"No—Kirk might lose his hold, and we don't know how deep the water is," Dr. Alston said. "Hurry with the lights. After you bring me those you can phone for help."

He had climbed back up, with Kirk hanging onto his neck, before the Rescue Squad got there, and all the excitement was over without even waking up the neighborhood. But it surprised me when Sherry started crying. I had never seen her cry before. She ran and hugged Kirk and then just stood there holding onto him till he twisted away from her—I think it scared him more than falling into the well, to see Sherry cry.

"What were you children doing out here this time of night?" Dr. Alston asked Sherry, but he didn't sound very angry—only as if he thought he had to.

"It was a dare. She dared us to look down in the well at midnight," Sherry sobbed.

"Who dared you? Not Lindsey?" Dr. Alston looked shocked.

"No, sir," I said emphatically. "I missed the boys and came to look for them, before Mama and Dad could find out they were gone. I was afraid they might have wandered down to the—" And then I stopped, not quite wanting to mention the pond.

"Who dared you, Sherry?"

Sherry looked so defenseless, standing there in front of us with her arm crooked over her face, that I couldn't help feeling sorry for her. But then she said, "Miranda—it was Miranda—" and I felt hardhearted again when I saw how shook up Dr. Alston and Miss Judith both looked. Of course Sherry's mother still thought Miranda was just her imaginary playmate. So she told Sherry she didn't want to hear any more about Miranda—that she needn't blame her naughtiness on a make-believe child any more, because they wouldn't stand for it. Sherry didn't argue, but Dr. Alston said kind of wearily, "Oh, now, Olivia, let's not be harsh."

When he said that, Sherry started crying even harder, and Dr. Alston tried to take her in his arms, but she wouldn't let him. She was fighting him and sobbing, "You don't care about *me*—you don't—" and Mrs. Alston had to almost carry her into the house. So I guess she wasn't punished after all, and maybe that was all right, because she probably didn't really mean any harm.

Mama and Dad had slept right through the excitement. So did the Greenfields. I told Tammy all about it the next day. "And I brought Eddie and Kirk home, and Mrs. Brer had Five and Six and Seven and Eight and Nine. Eddie ran ahead and looked. Kirk wasn't caring much about rabbits right then. He didn't want me to tell Mama and Dad about the well, so now he has to do anything I tell him to for the next three weeks. But Dr. Alston might let on to them."

"Well, I'd like to see Five and Six and Seven and Eight and Nine," Tammy said. I've never seen any rabbits that new." So we went and inspected them, and then went over and watched the workmen filling up and boarding over the old well. Dr.

Alston must have been really scared, to get them out there so quick.

We asked the workman who was down in the well (it wasn't really very full of water, after all) if he saw anything down there like a small lump of cement shaped like an owl with yellow glass eyes, but he didn't.

We went around to the side yard, then, and Miss Judith came out about that time, and asked if Kirk was all right. I said, "Yes, ma'am, but I'm surprised to find my hair hasn't turned white overnight, from the shock."

She said she thought she had a few more gray hairs that morning. Tammy said, "I wish I hadn't missed all the excitement."

"Never mind, there's bound to be some more," I told her. "Here comes Mr. Farrar. I think I'll ask him if we can come to the séance, just to see what he'll say. Mrs. Farrar must have the car again; he's walking home from the hardware store."

"How do you deduce that?"

"He's carrying a kind of heavy-looking brown paper sack with Greene Hardware Company printed on it." We both went off into giggles, and even Miss Judith was smiling when Mr. Farrar came along the sidewalk abreast of us.

I thought I'd start the conversation casually and then lead into the real question. "What're you making in your workshop now, Mr. Farrar? The flower-pots you made for Mrs. Farrar look great."

"Nothing." He really meant it was none of my business.

I composed my face to look serious. "Mr. Farrar, Tammy and I are very much interested in spiritualism, and we would like to be at the séance when you have it at her house. And I'm sure I'm psychic —I was born with two cauls, you see."

"Two cauls!" Mr. Farrar gasped, and Tammy nearly exploded trying to keep from laughing out loud. Maybe he actually believed it for a minute. It was all I could do to keep from saying I'd been born with eight fingers on each hand, too. "Maybe you are a sensitive, Lindsey, and sometime we'll have to explore that possibility. But not this time. It's possible to have only a very few serious psychic investigators at this meeting."

"Well, I'll be there anyway," I said solemnly, "if I should happen to die before Friday. You can count on me to get in touch with you through Kleeman."

"Lindsey—hush!" Miss Judith said. "You aren't going to die before Friday, child."

"Maybe I will," I said. "Tammy, too. We'd do anything to get to the séance. Do suicides ever Come Through?" I don't know how I managed to keep a straight face. Tammy just hid hers in her hands.

"Maybe she is clairvoyant," Mr. Farrar said to Miss Judith. "Do you have some kind of premonition, Lindsey?"

"I don't know what that is," I said innocently. "All I know is, I had a kind of mental picture—in technicolor—of me lying in a coffin. I could even feel how narrow it was. And there were flowers— pale pink carnations, I think—and music. Was that a premonition, Mr. Farrar?"

"Good heavens, child," was all he said to me. But he said to Miss Judith, "There *is* some evidence to prove clairvoyance. Dr. Rhine, you know—"

"She's joking, Mr. Farrar," Miss Judith said. "It's not a very funny joke, but you know how children are."

Mr. Farrar shook his head and went on across the street to his own house, and I called after him, "Please be sure to tell Kleeman I'll be there Friday night if I can, Mr. Farrar."

"Lindsey, you shouldn't!" Miss Judith said, shocked.

"I know it, Miss Judith," I said, after Tammy and I had recovered from laughing ourselves into a coughing spell. "I'm sorry, but I do hate Mr. Farrar, and it's fun putting him on."

"I wish you wouldn't joke about such things," Miss Judith said sadly, and then I really was sorry, and I tried to tell her I wouldn't have hurt her feelings for the world. She forgave me, but I could tell she still felt sad. "Well," she told us, "I have to go and straighten up Miranda's—I mean Sherry's —room, while she's out playing with Eddie and Kirk."

"They're looking at the new rabbits," Tammy told her. "You want us to go with you, Miss Judith? So you won't be lonely in Miranda's room?"

"Why, yes, if you want to, Tammy. That might be a good idea. You may turn out to know as much psychology as your father, some day. I'll admit I rather dread being in there, without Miranda." Or with Miranda, I couldn't help thinking.

Of course it wasn't kindness on Tammy's part— we had been dying to get into Miranda's room again. There might be clues there, clues to where the cement owl was hidden, or to where Sherry was getting all the stuff she knew about Miranda. Or we might be able to feel the eerie presence, if there really was a ghost child living there too.

We followed Miss Judith up the stairs, eagerly. The room she had fixed for Miranda was all pink and white, like strawberry ice cream and whipped cream, or like those mountain laurel flowers we saw once up in the hills.

"Some of the furniture in here was my mother's when she was a girl," Miss Judith said. "The rose-wood desk was, and that little rocking chair she used for a sewing chair. And then they were mine, when I was growing up."

"It's lovely," I said. "I wish I had real antiques in my room."

Miss Judith opened the desk—it had a top that folded down on hinges—to show us the inside. There were lots of pigeonholes, and a little drawer in the middle. "There's a secret place behind this drawer," she said. "Well, not so very secret—it's just a deeper space behind the drawer than it really needs, which doesn't show unless you take the drawer all the way out. I loved hiding things there, when I was a child. So did Miranda. I haven't showed it to Sherry, yet."

But before she could take out the drawer for us to see behind it, she noticed something lying flat on the polished surface under the pigeonholes. "Why—she found these, too!" she exclaimed.

"What is it?" Tammy said.

There were two books lying there, an ABC book with colored pictures, and *A Child's Garden of Verses* by Robert Louis Stevenson. "These weren't here," Miss Judith said with that strange tone in her voice that I was getting used to, "before Sherry came. I don't know where she found them. I haven't seen them since Miranda was here. She loved these two books—I never knew what became of them."

She opened the poetry book to the flyleaf, and I could see what was written there. "'For Miranda, with all my love, from Mother." I didn't have to look in the other one; I knew it said the same thing.

"Her mother gave them to her," Tammy said unnecessarily. "The lady who was interested in spiritualism."

"I wonder where Sherry found them—if Sherry found them—?" Miss Judith murmured.

"I know!" I said. "Remember, Tammy? Eddie said when they found the place that had been dug out in the summer house, when Sherry fell into it, there were some other things in it besides the old carnival whip. Some money in a baking-powder can, and some old beat-up books in a tin box. These must be the books. That was where Miranda hid her treasures."

"But not the cement owl," Tammy reminded me.

"Well, she probably had other hiding places."

"Did Eddie say how many books there were?" Miss Judith asked.

"No, he didn't. I can ask him. But I doubt if he'd remember. Eddie's not terribly interested in books right now. Unless they're about raising rabbits. Or comic books, of course. Did she have more books, Miss Judith?"

"I don't know," Miss Judith said. "She might have. She had a little diary—" She put the books carefully back in the desk, where she had found them. "That's right where she used to keep them," she almost whispered. I could tell she was thinking that maybe it was Miranda who put them there, not Sherry at all. "She used to sit here and write."

Tammy was getting impatient, and I was anxious, too, to see the secret place in Miranda's desk. "You were going to show us the secret place behind the drawer," I said gently.

"Oh, yes." Miss Judith came back from the past, almost. "This is the way it works." She started to take out the drawer.

"You said you never showed this to Sherry?" I asked, wondering if the child might have found something there, something she was using to mystify us. That diary, for instance.

"I never did, Lindsey. I didn't want Sherry to have the same experiences with me that Miranda had; so I didn't tell her about the secret place. We used to leave notes for each other there, Miranda and I." I remembered she had said something like that before, about not wanting to do the same things with the two of them.

"But Sherry might have found the secret place on her own."

Miss Judith took out the drawer and laid it on the desk's writing surface, shaking her head. "No, I don't think anyone would suspect there was a secret hole back there, do you?" she said. "Not unless there was some reason to take the drawer all the way out."

"Oh, kids always take things apart," I told her, knowing Eddie and Kirk.

We all leaned over and peered into the dark place where the drawer had been.

There was something in it.

"Look!" That was Tammy.

"What is it?" That was me.

Miss Judith turned white, then she steadied herself and said faintly, "I haven't looked in there for years, not since—"

Almost fearfully, while Tammy and I held our breaths, she put her trembling hand into the secret hole.

7

DAME PYTHIA
ARRIVES

The piece of paper was sort of scrappy, but only slightly yellow. "Dear Aunt Judith," it said, "I love you." It wasn't signed.

Had Miranda written it, long ago? Or—can ghosts write?

Or had Sherry written it, just the other day? I remembered the blue rose. Had Sherry wanted Miss Judith to think it was Miranda's ghost who had left the note there? At least, to think so at first? Or had Sherry just been making another pitiful attempt to make her aunt love her the way she had Miranda? Maybe she honestly didn't realize how it would make Miss Judith feel. And Sherry had told her aunt she fixed the blue rose, as soon as the subject came up. She might admit writing the note, too, when she was asked. There was no need to sign it, of course, when only one child with an "Aunt Judith" was—supposedly—in the house.

Miss Judith's hands were shaky, and there were

tears in her eyes. She must think Miranda wrote it, I thought, feeling sad for her. "Miss Judith," I said softly, "does it look like Sherry's writing?"

"It must be Miranda's," she said faintly. "She must have written it all those years ago."

"But could it be Sherry's writing?" I kept at her, though I was sorry for her. "You're her Aunt Judith too. And the paper doesn't look too old."

"Old enough, though," Tammy said.

"I don't know," Miss Judith said. "I haven't seen much of Sherry's writing. And it's a long time since I saw Miranda's. I honestly can't tell which it is."

"Let's find Sherry and ask her," Tammy suggested. Miss Judith went with us to the rabbit cages.

Eddie said, "I gave Seven to Sherry. But he has to stay with his mother until he's weaned."

Sherry said, sighing hopefully at her Aunt Judith, "I did want a horse, but I guess a rabbit's better than nothing."

"Yep," Kirk said.

"Well, if you don't want Seven—" Eddie said, a bit indignantly.

"Oh, I want him, all right. I'm going to name him Nightmare."

"He's not black."

"Well, there could be a sort of grayish Nightmare, couldn't there? Like a black-and-white dream instead of technicolor? And then if I ever do get a horse named Nightmare, I can change my bunny's name back to Seven."

"Well, okay," Eddie said a little doubtfully.

I broke into their silly yakety-yak to ask, casually, "Sherry, when did you write this note to your Aunt Judith?" I read in a psychology magazine that the way to find out if a child did anything isn't to say "Did you?" but "When did you?" I've been on my guard ever since.

"Oh, did you find it, Aunt Judith?" Sherry smiled affectionately at her aunt; you'd have sworn there was nothing tricky about her. Just like the time she admitted the blue rose was a surprise for poor Miss Judith. "I was wondering if you ever would. I wrote it two days ago, and I thought you'd never look in the secret place."

"How did you know about the desk?" Miss Judith asked, and it was pitiful, the way she looked at Sherry, pleading, "Dear, please tell me—"

"*You* know who," Sherry said. "Mom said not to mention her name anymore."

Miss Judith got very pale. "Don't look like that, Miss Judith," I said. "Sherry's probably just making it up. You know she was just fooling around the desk and happened to find the secret place."

"Yes, that's right; I just happened to find it, Aunt Judith," Sherry said, in that innocent-slippery tone of voice kids use when they want people to think they're telling a whopper even if it happens to be the truth. It's a good way to tell the truth and still have all the advantages of lying. It was working right now, on Miss Judith. But *I* didn't believe Sherry found out from Miranda—she looked too much like a kitten playing with a dead bird.

"Well," Miss Judith said uncertainly, "it's a sweet note, Sherry, and—thank you, dear."

"Aunt Judith," Sherry said, looking up through her bangs in that weird way she had, "why didn't you tell me about the secret place in the desk? Or any of the other things you told Miranda?"

Well, that was a poser. I could tell Miss Judith didn't know what to say, because really there wasn't any good answer, even if Dr. Alston had left her free to tell, and he hadn't

Miss Judith answered weakly, after awhile, with another question. "Who—do you think Miranda is, Sherry?"

Sherry flitted away, like an elfish imp, calling back over her shoulder. "Don't you know? Don't you know? She's my make-believe sister, that's who!"

Yes, any imaginative kid might have said it. Whether she knew the facts about Miranda or not. And whether Miranda was a real ghost or not.

Eddie latched the rabbit cage and he and Kirk hurried off after Sherry.

"Don't let her bug you, Miss Judith," Tammy said kindly.

"She's such a mysterious child," Miss Judith sighed. "If I believed in reincarnation, I might wonder if Miranda had been re-born as Sherry. They look so much alike. Sherry was born two years after Miranda died. So it would have been possible, if reincarnation is possible."

"But you don't believe in it?" I asked Miss Judith. "You mean the Psychic Society doesn't go in for reincarnation?"

"I don't know what to believe," Miss Judith said, sort of desperately.

"Well, one thing's for sure," I told her, "you can't believe Miranda is in communication with Sherry and still believe she's reincarnated in Sherry. It'll have to be one or the other, won't it? So I guess you have to decide which is the least weird, huh, Miss Judith? Or else not believe in any of it, and decide Sherry is making it all up, getting her knowledge about Miranda from something—or someone—we don't know about."

"I suppose so," Miss Judith murmured, but she sounded doubtful still. "Anyway, I'll know in a couple of days. The séance is Friday night. If nothing comes through from Miranda, with Dame Pythia and Kleeman trying, then I'll stop believing she's able to communicate."

She wanted so much to believe it that I wished it could be true. I hoped Dame Pythia and Kleeman were really in touch with The Other World. But at the same time I was mad at Mr. Farrar for trying to get publicity at the expense of Miss Judith's feelings. I hoped something would happen at the séance that would scare him to death—maybe Tammy and I could think up something.

When Friday came, we were out front watching for Dame Pythia to arrive at the Farrars'. We had seen her picture in the Atlanta papers, and in *Time* and *Life* magazines too, so we weren't surprised at how fat she was. But we had no idea what a funny color of pinkish-orange her hair would turn out to be. And she wore blue stretch-pants that were really stretched, and a kind of long tunic in all sorts of psychedelic colors. While we were watching her get out of Mr. Farrar's car, Sherry and Eddie and Kirk came around from the backyard, and all five of us strolled across the street and said "Hello" to both of them. Mr. Farrar said, "Hello, children," very grudgingly, but Dame Pythia said, holding out her hands like she was sleep-walking, "Vibrations! Vibrations! There are sensitives here!"

I said, "I was born with two cauls," just to see what she'd say, and she grabbed me by my shoulders and said, "Ah," just as if a doctor had told her to say it while he held a little flat stick on her tongue. She must have guessed I was putting her on about the two cauls, because she didn't react beyond the "ah."

She looked at Sherry and Mr. Farrar said, "This is Sherry Alston, Dame Pythia," and Sherry said, "How do you do," quite nicely. Dame Pythia turned me loose and grabbed Sherry by the shoulders and looked deep into her eyes. Sherry squirmed, and Dame Pythia let her go and nodded significantly to Mr. Farrar. He said, "She's the little girl I was telling you about." I knew he had introduced Sherry instead of the rest of us because she was important to the plot. But we didn't like to be ignored. I said, "I'm Lindsey Morrow, and this is my friend Tammy Greenfield. You are going to her house for the séance tonight; her father is Dr. Greenfield. These are my brothers, Eddie and Kirk."

Dame Pythia didn't bother about manners; she latched onto Tammy and ignored the rest of us. "Tammy," she said, tasting the name as if it were raspberry syrup. "When is your birthday, child?"

"February fifth," Tammy said, and I nearly giggled, because it wasn't—that was Kirk's birthday. "I'm a child of Aquarius." She isn't; her birthday's in September, just about a month before mine. She was trying to see just how psychic Dame Pythia could be when somebody was putting her on. And Kirk helped by saying, "Yep."

"Ah," Dame Pythia said again. "Ethical, idealistic, a lover of truth—" and then I did giggle. "Uranus is the planet which rules Aquarians, the

99

planet of progress and of truth. And when were your father and mother born, Tammy?"

Of course Tammy knew Dame Pythia was pumping her for stuff to use that night, in case she decided to try anything on Dr. Greenfield. "Daddy's birthday is June twentieth," she said innocently, "and Mother's is August thirteenth." So I was sure they weren't. Well, I believe white lies are justified when you're trying to help somebody like Miss Judith by showing up a person who's trying to hurt her.

"Do you remember your grandma, dear?"

"Of course," Tammy said, wide-eyed. She bravely blinked back tears and wiped her eyes on the back of her hand. Both her grandmothers are still alive, but you'd never have guessed it. "I was six when she died. Her first name was May, just like my middle name." Well, I hadn't heard about that, but knowing Tammy, I was pretty sure she had just changed her grandma's name. And Tammy herself had never had a middle name at all, she told me a long time ago.

I wondered why Dame Pythia wasn't asking Sherry some questions, to help in fooling Dr. Alston and Miss Judith. I found out later why—she already knew enough about the Alstons. And of course she didn't care a hoot about me and Eddie and Kirk—our parents weren't going to be at the séance.

Tammy said, "Dame Pythia, could Lindsey and I please come to the séance? We're very interested in psychic things."

Sherry said quickly, "If you'll let me come, I'll bring Miranda." She was supposed to spend the night at our house, sleeping in my room while I was over at Tammy's, because her mother had gone to Atlanta, and her father and aunt might be very late getting home from the séance.

Mr. Farrar said crossly, "No. As I told you before, girls, the meeting isn't for children."

Dame Pythia said to him, "Perhaps she *is* in touch—"

But Mr. Farrar said curtly, "Impossible." So he *knew* there was nothing to it! It proved to me he didn't believe in any of it—not even in trance mediums—or he'd at least have thought *maybe* Sherry could communicate with Miranda through Dame Pythia.

Sherry ran off, calling back, "Then Miranda won't come! She'll stay with me! You won't hear from Miranda at your silly old séance!"

It really sounded as if she believed it. As if there really were a Miranda she was in communication with. She must have overheard some talk of the séance at home, and she may have even guessed by now who Miranda was. She'd have to be pretty stupid not to.

Kirk and Eddie ran after Sherry, and Tammy

and I went on to her house, giggling all the way down to our toes. When nobody was looking we inspected the hall closet, and it was all ready for our knothole view of the séance. The dug-out holes were still wide open, which goes to show that their maid, Theolia, doesn't dust behind those chairs very well, or she'd have noticed them. We could see nearly the whole room when the lights were on. At that moment Dr. Greenfield was moving the couch from his study into the middle of the room, for Dame Pythia to lie on, and we hoped it would hold up under the strain. He hoped so too, we heard him telling Mrs. Greenfield while they were setting up extra bridge chairs around it.

"There's just no chance for any trick stuff here," he went on, in a satisfied voice. "Sometimes, you know, they apparently materialize objects from The Other World—but we know they can't do it in our living room. They'd have to have wires rigged up, or magicians' apparatus or projection machines or something."

"I don't think," Mrs. Greenfield answered, "from what I've read, that Dame Pythia does any of what they call 'external manifestations.'" Her voice sounded as if she might be laughing to herself. "Perhaps she's too lazy to make the effort. I think she relies entirely on Kleeman and his extraordinary knowledge of the victim and his contact on The Other Side."

"You're right, but we want to rule out any possibility of trickery."

It was all very exciting. Tammy and I could hardly wait for eight o'clock that night, when everybody was supposed to meet. I was eating at the Greenfield's; they had fried chicken, which Theolia really knows how to cook—it's the greatest. But we were so excited we could hardly eat a thing except two drumsticks apiece, and some biscuits and honey, and apple pie and ice cream. Theolia is a genius at making apple pie, too. We didn't have a bit of room for the salad and green vegetables.

We got excused as soon as we finished the ice cream, and went up to Tammy's room, which is a corner one with a window at the front and one at the side—we had a great view in both directions. It was nearly eight, but still twilight. Cars kept coming until the street was lined with them. Somebody must have told some others, because more than ten people got out of the cars.

"Look," Tammy said. "Here comes Dame Pythia across the street with Mrs. Farrar."

"Wonder where Mr. Farrar is?" As president of the group, he certainly wouldn't be late for the séance.

Then I saw him. He was acting odd, furtive-like. He went out the back door of his house, and hurried on down the alley out of sight.

But in a few minutes Tammy said, "Here comes

Mr. Farrar now." He was coming from the direction of my house—or he could have gone beyond
that to the Alstons', I thought. It was very peculiar,
to say the least.

"Put on the records," I said. "The cars have
stopped coming, and now that Mr. Farrar's here,
the fun should begin."

Tammy put twelve records on, fairly loud, so
they could be heard downstairs, but not loud
enough for her mother to call and tell her to cut
down the noise.

Then, holding our breaths and not making a
sound, we crept down the stairs and shut ourselves
into the hall closet. There was plenty of room, because since it was summer only raincoats were
hanging there now.

What if Miranda were really able to "communicate" tonight—not through Dame Pythia and Kleeman, but in some other way? I felt chilly all of a
sudden, in that stuffy, airless closet.

And Tammy—the girl who didn't believe in
ghosts—whispered, "Lindsey, it's cold in here, isn't
it?"

8

THE SEANCE

"I'm almost shivering," I whispered back. "How could it be cold in a stuffy closet on a hot night?"

"We've got to be imagining it," Tammy mumbled. "Let's take a look through the holes."

I spotted Dame Pythia at once. She was meeting all the members, and saying ordinary things to them, just as if she weren't a famous medium. Then Mr. Farrar said, "Well! Shall we get started?" Everybody found a chair and settled down, as close as they could decently get to the couch. Mrs. Farrar was fussing with the tape recorder, which was on a table at the end of the couch, where Dame Pythia's head would be. Mrs. Farrar must have been elected to get everything on tape, to check it out later.

Mr. Farrar made a little speech, about how lucky they were to have Dame Pythia with them, and thanked Dr. and Mrs. Greenfield for inviting the Society to have the séance at their house.

Dr. Greenfield said graciously, "We are most

interested. Now is there anything further we should do in preparation?"

"Well, we usually have only a dim light," Mr. Farrar said. "Discarnates seem to shun the brighter lights, and we want to attract as many of them as possible."

"Discarnates" was a new word to us, but I guessed it was another name for ghosts.

When Dr. Greenfield turned out all the lights but one, everybody stopped talking and looked at Dame Pythia. She was sitting on the edge of the couch, which made it sag.

"I have no idea," she said, "what we'll get tonight. Sometimes they come, from The Other Side, and then again they don't. If anything happens, it will happen because of you people, not because of me. It will be because there's someone Over There who wants to communicate with you. I can't bring them. Kleeman can't bring them. But if they come, Kleeman will put you in touch with them.

"Often what they say will seem trivial to you—but most conversations between the living are trivial, aren't they? Why should discarnates be different? And if the details seem not to be anything you can recognize, make a note of them and check it out later. You'll find there is often something in the conversation that will prove the entities on The Other Side still live, still remember the ones they loved while here.

"I will not be conscious, of course, of anything that happens while I am in the trance state; Kleeman takes over my body. Ask him any questions you wish. Remember, he can't bring anybody back; he can only describe the ones who are trying to get through to you. You will have to do the recognizing."

She tied a white silk scarf over her eyes, and stretched out on the couch, crossing her ankles. Then she seemed to fall asleep. There wasn't enough light for Tammy and me to see her too well, but enough to see her stomach in the psychedelic tunic rising and falling as she breathed.

There was a breathless hush, and I even heard the click as Mrs. Farrar turned on the tape recorder.

Then a man's heavy voice coming from Dame Pythia said, "Guten Abend. Goot eefning. I am Kleeman."

Nobody laughed. A lot of them said politely, "Good evening, Kleeman," just as if he were real. I was watching Miss Judith and Dr. Alston. Miss Judith had answered Kleeman, but neither Dr. Alston nor Dr. Greenfield spoke.

I won't try to do Kleeman's German accent—it sounded as if he were trying to clear his throat, and he turned sentences around so the last part came first. Once in a while, though, he forgot to use his accent. I wondered if any of the Society members noticed that. They were all too busy telling Kleeman the things he was fishing to find out.

"Someone there is here," he said, "trying to get across, someone whose name begins with J—"

"My brother Jack," one lady said eagerly. "Is it Jack?"

"Does anyone know a John?" Kleeman said. "I can't quite get it—it is something about an automobile accident—"

"I had a friend named Jim who was in an automobile accident," another lady said. "But I didn't know it killed him. Is it Jim? If it's Jim, ask him to tell me his dog's name. That would be something evidential."

"Ach, it is fading," Kleeman said regretfully. "Now comes a lady who was close to someone in this room."

Tammy nudged me, and we had a hard time keeping from exploding.

"Now a calendar I see—her first name has something to do with this calendar," Kleeman said solemnly. "The months are passing—one, two, three, four, five—here it stops."

"May!" one of the ladies cried. "Her name must have been May!"

Dr. Greenfield didn't say anything and neither did Mrs. Greenfield, which must have puzzled Dame Pythia considerably, since they were supposed to recognize her. Kleeman sounded disappointed. "This lady nobody recognizes?"

He changed the subject abruptly. "Comes now somebody named George. Does anybody know George?"

"If it's my great uncle George," a lady said hopefully, "he can tell me what kind of tree he planted at my house just before he died."

George didn't respond to that. Kleeman said, "Medicine it is about—too much medicine—he was a long time sick? Or maybe an overdose?"

"I don't know," the lady murmured uncertainly. "I'll check it out. Maybe it's evidential."

"Someone in the room," Kleeman said, "has a birthday in June?" Several people admitted it, but

Dr. Greenfield wasn't one of them. "Somebody comes for this gentleman—somebody with an M—" He wasn't going to give up on May, not knowing she wasn't really Dr. Greenfield's mother—whose name, I found out later, was Rebekah. Tammy and I smothered our giggles. One of the June ladies said, "I have a sister Mary—but she's still on the earth plane, as far as I know." She looked a little scared, as if May might have died in the past five minutes and this was how she was getting the news.

"A soldier comes," Kleeman went on. That was a pretty fair possibility—almost everybody knows of some soldier in the family who was killed in some war, and Kleeman hadn't said yet what kind of uniform the discarnate was wearing.

"What color is his hair?" Mrs. Farrar whispered. I remembered hearing Mama say that Mrs. Farrar's father had been killed in World War II, and I felt sorry for her. "If he has red hair, that would be evidential."

Kleeman was too cagey to make it red. "Not clear is his head. It might be a hat—or bandages—"

"He got a head wound!" Mrs. Farrar said. "Oh, it's Father! Oh, if only he could speak to me!" If she hadn't spoken up, I guess Kleeman would have put the bandage on the discarnate's leg or some other place, so somebody else would claim him.

Kleeman said, "He tells you he comes through as he died, so as to be recognized, but that Over

There is no pain felt. He has transcended his bodily ills. He says to tell you all is beautiful where he is, and do not be sad."

Mrs. Farrar murmured, "Thank you, Father—I'm so glad!" and I felt sorry for her again. Because she really is quite nice. It's just that we can't see how she can stand being married to Mr. Farrar. And somebody ought to explain to her about immortality so she wouldn't have to feed people like Dame Pythia in order not to have to worry about her poor father's soul, which is sure to be okay unless he was a murderer or something, and even then I'm not certain it wouldn't, because maybe it's not a murderer's fault if he's that way.

Kleeman brought in a few more very vague discarnates that some of the people thought might be evidential if they checked them out—one lady was going to ask her aunt if her mother had ever had a cat named Macbeth because if she had, that was surely her mother trying to get through.

And then Kleeman really got down to business. He began to sing, just a snatch of a Shakespeare song, and anything less like Ariel's voice would be hard to imagine. "*—doth suffer a sea-change into something rich and strange—*" he growled. I elbowed Tammy. We had *The Tempest* last year in English. "Miranda," she whispered back.

"Comes now a small child," Kleeman said. "Hovers near—trying to reach a lady in this room

—and a man. The name begins with N . . . or
. . . I can't see clearly—it's misty there—no, it's
M."

"Miranda!" Mrs. Farrar cried out, and then
clapped her hand over her mouth. I can't believe
she knew what they were up to. She reached over
and patted Miss Judith's hand so kindly and sym-
pathetically.

"Is it a—girl child?" Miss Judith asked faintly.

Dr. Alston on her other side said fiercely, "Wait,
Judith! Don't say anything at all!"

Kleeman said solemnly, "I cannot tell. It is too
cloudy there. But yes, she nods. You are both
right. It is a little girl. She wants someone in this
room to remember a—a little book, a little leather
book—a present, a Christmas present—"

Mrs. Farrar said excitedly, "I remember! It *is*
Miranda! I gave her a diary for Christmas—that
last Christmas before—remember, Judith? I gave
her the little blue leather diary. She told me she
wrote in it every night."

Miss Judith said in a choked-with-tears voice,
"I do remember. I thought of it when I found the
other books in her desk, where she sat and wrote in
the diary."

But Dr. Alston looked suspiciously at Mr. Farrar
and said, "Do you remember it too, Mr. Farrar?"
and Mr. Farrar said he didn't, but of course he did.
That had to be how Kleeman found out.

I nudged Tammy and she whispered, "Sherry found it! That would explain lots of things." But did Miranda's ghost show Sherry where she hid the diary? Miss Judith hadn't found it in all those years.

Kleeman went on, "There is here someone who loved this child, who does not believe she comes back from The Other Side. For him she has this word which will mean nothing to any other person here. It is a strange word. I do not this word myself know. 'C-o-o-t.' Does it mean anything to anyone here?"

Dr. Alston gasped and leaped to his feet. "What *is* this?" he shouted. "Where did you get that?"

Kleeman was silent. Dame Pythia didn't stir.

"Do you know the word, Dr. Alston?" Mr. Farrar asked.

"William!" Miss Judith said. "Do you? Was it something you and Miranda knew? I never heard it myself. William, can it be—Miranda?"

"No!" Dr. Alston said firmly. "It's a pet name I called Miranda when she was a baby. You weren't living near us then, Judith. This is some kind of a trick. Miranda wouldn't have remembered the name; she was too small when I stopped using it."

"All is revealed when we get to The Other Side," Mr. Farrar said. "She would know it now. But nobody in this room knew it except you, Dr. Alston?"

Dr. Alston sat down again. "All right," he said grimly. "What else do you know?"

"She says," Kleeman grunted, "you to remind —something about a seashell with a name written on it and a silver knife with paint drippings from it —and an alligator's tooth."

Dr. Alston groaned, and put his head in his hands. Miss Judith said slowly, almost fearfully, "I remember you punished her once when I was there, when she was very small, for putting one of the good silver knives in a can of green paint. Oh, Miranda! My little Miranda! Is it you?"

It was clearly what they all thought "evidential." And Dr. Alston as clearly recognized the seashell and the alligator's tooth, too. Those weren't things that could happen to everybody, like automobile accidents.

I felt colder and colder.

Then Kleeman said, "The child tells about a bird. A bird—heavy—not to fly—made of something heavy—a bird with yellow eyes. An owl, that's it—"

Miss Judith gasped, "The owl! Oh, if she can tell me where to find the owl, that will really prove it's Miranda. Nobody knows where she hid it. She told me she didn't even write it down in her diary, because it was such a secret. Tell me, Miranda— you were going to tell me for my birthday, remember?"

114

Kleeman's voice said, "She is fading . . . she has to go . . . she must hurry to tell—she says to look under four bricks at the edge of—of the . . . Is there water? Lake or pond?"

"Yes!" Miss Judith said. "There's the pond. She might have been arranging those four bricks when she fell in! Oh, William, if it's there, if only it's there, we'll know!"

There was what the books call "an electric silence" in the room, while Dame Pythia's stomach rose and fell with her heavy breathing.

Then Tammy sneezed.

9

THE CLUE IN
THE DESK

Well, the sneeze didn't exactly break up the séance—I guess Kleeman was getting pretty tired of talking with that German accent anyhow. But Tammy's mother came looking for us when she heard the sneeze. Kleeman was saying, "Gute Nacht. Goot night," and everybody said, "Goodnight, Kleeman," and then Dame Pythia sat up heavily, creaking the couch, and said in her ordinary voice, "Did anything evidential happen?" As if she didn't know.

Then Mrs. Greenfield found us, and we had to go up to bed. We didn't even get any of the refreshments that we had planned to sneak upstairs before they got around to their coffee.

We had set Tammy's alarm clock for five, because we wanted to get up at daylight and go dig for the owl, and you couldn't very well do that in the dark. Even Miss Judith and Dr. Alston wouldn't be that foolish, we figured. But we were pretty sleepy, and could barely open our eyes, even with the alarm clock ringing its head off.

"Turn it off," Tammy mumbled. "Mother'll hear it."

"It's your clock," I said. But I did it, because it was on my side of the bed. I was more awake than Tammy; so it was my responsibility to get us up and not let us go back to sleep. "Come on, Tam," I said firmly. "On your feet. We've got to go and dig up the owl, remember? And then we'll know whether that was really Miranda who showed up last night."

She was pretty reluctant, but we both were wide awake after I washed my face and tried to wash hers and we had a scuffle over the washrag. Then we dressed in a hurry and tiptoed downstairs without waking her parents.

It was a foggy morning. Everything was so gray we could scarcely see. We went cautiously across my backyard—not making any noise because we didn't want the boys and Sherry to wake up and get in on the search—and stopped only a minute to say hello to Mrs. Brer and the babies. She was twitching her nose at us, and so was Brer over in his separate cage. We didn't stop to feed them— we were too excited about the cement owl. Just suppose we find it under those bricks, I thought— that means ghosts are real. My skin prickled.

We heard voices before we saw who was talking.

Dr. Alston and Miss Judith were just ahead of us, walking down to the pond—he was carrying a shovel. I pulled Tammy back, and she nodded. Maybe they oughtn't to know we were there. Maybe we ought to let them find the owl. After all, Miranda was their little ghost.

But we had to see what happened. So we followed, very quietly.

Dr. Alston was saying firmly, "Judith, we simply must keep this in mind: whatever it is at work here, it is not Miranda. Now you must stop believing it was Miranda. I am not convinced."

"You said you might be if anything evidential happened," she said plaintively, "and it did. You recognized things nobody knew but you—not even I knew about the pet name. I did know about the silver knife with the paint, and the seashell you brought her from the beach, and the alligator tooth she cut her teeth on, but Dame Pythia didn't. It's really evidential, William."

"Farrar remembered that his wife gave Miranda the diary. The medium used that for openers. And by the way, what became of the diary?"

"I've been trying to remember if I saw it, when I put her things away. I was still in shock then, you know. You said you didn't want to see any of them—and I didn't either. So I put all her clothes and toys and little things in a heavy pasteboard box and stored them in the attic. I can't remember if I saw the diary then or not. I was just trying to get through the task as well as I could, as quickly as I could. It might be there."

"We'll look, after we find this cement owl under these four mythical bricks."

"If the owl is there, William, you'll have to admit we were really in touch with Miranda last night," Miss Judith pleaded.

"If it is, I'll be very much surprised," Dr. Alston said, as if he wasn't the least bit worried about having to admit it.

But he had sounded a bit doubtful about those other things, the things Miss Judith had called "evidential." They weren't easy for any skeptic to explain away.

Now they had reached the edge of the pond. "We'll have to walk around it, I suppose," Dr. Alston grumbled, "until we come to four bricks. If we ever do."

"Be careful," Miss Judith said automatically. Then she gave a little gasp. "Why, look, William! There's some bricks! Old mossy ones. Four, if you count nearly whole ones."

"And," Dr. Alston said with more excitement than he had shown yet, "something was buried under them. There's a hole. An empty hole. Dug recently, not an old one."

Miss Judith was so disappointed she sat right

down on an old tree stump and started to cry. "Oh, William! Somebody took it. Now we'll never know."

Dr. Alston started digging in the empty hole, but we could tell he didn't expect to find anything. "No use," he said after awhile. "Somebody beat us to it, all right. Now why would anybody—?"

"Nobody knew about it," Miss Judith wailed, "except the people who were there last night, and they all wanted us to get in touch with Miranda. They all hoped it would check out and prove she was really there. They wouldn't have stolen it."

"There's something very strange about this whole thing," Dr. Alston said. "I'd like to talk to this Dame Pythia when she's not in a trance."

"Oh, I'm afraid you can't, William. She was catching an early plane. Mr. Farrar was going to take her to the airport about four this morning. He's probably back by now. She left her New York address though, for you to get in touch with her if you wanted her to try to communicate further with Miranda. Do let her, William. She might tell us who dug up the owl."

I could have made a pretty good guess at that myself, if only there had been any way Sherry could have known what went on at the séance.

"Well," Dr. Alston said, "come on, Judith. Let's go and check the box in the attic, because if there was a diary anywhere and Sherry found it, some of the details she knew that bothered you could be explained. The ones Dame Pythia knew, of course, are a little harder to account for."

"But Miranda told me she didn't write in the diary where she had the owl with the golden eyes," Miss Judith reminded him, "because it was such a special secret. She wrote about how we made it, but not where she hid it."

"Let's look for the diary, anyway."

Tammy and I were already halfway up in the magnolia tree before they got as far as the summer house. We hoped they had left the attic windows open because of the heat, and sure enough, they had. We were snug and quiet in the branches next to that window long before Miss Judith and Dr. Alston had climbed the stairs. We could hear them open the door and fumble for the lights, and then we could hear them talking.

"Here's the box," Miss Judith said. "Why— William, it's been disturbed. It's not the way I left it, I'm sure. I always tape boxes shut a certain way. This one has had the tape broken and then stuck back together."

"It was so long ago, you might have done it yourself and then forgotten about it, if you found something else to put in after taping it. But it could have been Sherry, I guess. I'll ask her. If she says she didn't do it, what then? Judith, I confess I sometimes feel just—just helpless with Sherry.

It must be that I'm soft with her, because of Miranda. I let her get away with too much."

"I know how you feel," Miss Judith said. "I feel the same way. We ought to be firmer with her."

"Maybe Olivia can," Dr. Alston said.

"William, I tell you, we ought to tell Olivia about Miranda. Somehow I have a feeling that that's what Miranda wants—to be acknowledged. To have you tell Olivia and Sherry about your other little daughter. And have you carry her picture in your wallet along with Sherry's, and have me put her picture in the living room again. She might not be such a restless spirit, then."

"Now, Judith, you know Miranda is beyond wanting anything," Dr. Alston said sorrowfully. "Here, can you to bear to look through this box? I'll open it and we'll see if the diary is in it."

After a few minutes Miss Judith said, sounding as if she were crying, "I remember how she looked in that little flowered dress. Oh, William, I can't do it. Shut the box."

"There's no diary here," Dr. Alston said. "Did you look in the desk in her room—in the secret place in Mother's old desk?"

"Yes. There was only the note Sherry wrote, that nearly gave me heart failure. But of course, if Sherry found the diary, she hid it again. Very cleverly. We may never know whether she has been getting her knowledge from it, or from her 'make-believe sister.' "

"I'll try to make her tell me if she found the diary."

I could have told Sherry's father he wouldn't succeed. But he'd find that out. We saw the lights go out in the attic, and when we heard the door close, we rushed down out of the tree and went back to Tammy's for breakfast.

Dr. Greenfield was finishing his coffee, and he and Mrs. Greenfield had evidently decided to go easy on us for listening in on the séance the night before, because they smiled at us. Or maybe they were just finishing laughing. "Well, girls," he said, "after hearing the 'evidence,' do you have any more reason for believing the dead communicate with the living, than you had before?"

"Not exactly, sir," I said, "especially since Kleeman tried to fool you with some stuff Tammy told Dame Pythia about her grandma's name being May, and all that. But, Dr. Greenfield, somebody dug up the cement owl before we could check it out—before even Dr. Alston and Miss Judith could check it out." And while we ate about a dozen pancakes apiece we told him about the hole where the bricks had been.

"This is puzzling," he agreed. "If you find the answer, let me know."

"How about you, sir?" I asked. "Did you find

any evidence to prove anything about ghosts one way or the other? Do you think Miranda was there last night?"

"No," Dr. Greenfield said. "Candidly, Lindsey, I don't. But I'll be interested to hear what you girls turn up, about the explanation of all those 'evidential' bits that only Dr. Alston could have known about."

"If you were going to investigate it scientifically," I asked him, "how would you go about it?"

Dr. Greenfield lit his pipe and considered. "I suppose," he said thoughtfully, "assuming I believed the medium was a fraud, I'd try to find out where she could possibly have gotten the information which apparently no one but the victim knew."

Something had been bothering me in the back of my head, about that desk with the secret place in it, ever since Dr. Alston had mentioned it to Miss Judith, and it wasn't the diary or the note I was thinking about. Now, what Dr. Greenfield said somehow made things click into place. That "light bulb" you read about suddenly turned on, and I shouted, "Whee! I've got it! That's it! Tammy— Dr. Greenfield—I know now where Dame Pythia found out about the seashell and the alligator tooth and everything."

"Where?" Tammy demanded, but I said, "No time to explain now. We've got to hurry and catch Mr. Farrar before he leaves for his office. I've got to try my psychology trick on him and see if I'm right."

I grabbed Tammy and rushed her out, with her mouth still full of pancakes.

Dr. Greenfield said, "I think I'd better go with you." I didn't tell him not to, but I didn't wait for him, either.

10

THE OWL WITH
THE GOLDEN EYES

Mr. Farrar was just opening his garage when we got there, with Dr. Greenfield right behind us. Since it was a double garage, he had his workshop in there too, where he made things with all that stuff he was always getting from Greene's Hardware Store.

He was about to get into his car and drive off.

"Good morning, Mr. Farrar," I said.

"Morning." He wasn't too friendly, as usual.

"Did Dame Pythia catch the plane all right?" Dr. Greenfield said.

"Oh, she decided to stay another day and see if Dr. Alston wouldn't like to try another sitting. The results last night were spectacular—don't you agree, Dr. Greenfield?"

"I was—impressed," Dr. Greenfield said.

"I was, too, sir," I told Mr. Farrar innocently, "but we were wondering when you knew the first Mrs. Alston?"

He fell right in the trap, probably because he was impatient to get rid of me and get away.

"In New York. Why?"

"At the Psychic Society meeting, of course?" I said sweetly. "She was trying to get in touch with Miranda too? We knew from Miss Judith that Miranda's mother was interested in psychic things. Did she have a sitting with Dame Pythia? Did Kleeman tell her anything evidential?" I asked eagerly.

"Of course. But what's it to you, Lindsey? I'm in a hurry—if you'll excuse me, Dr. Greenfield," and he got into his car. Then he leaned across as he backed out, to say casually, "Oh, by the way, Doctor, have you heard if the Alstons found the owl?"

"It wasn't there," Dr. Greenfield said, watching him keenly. "They found the four bricks all right, but there was nothing under them."

"There had to be!" Mr. Farrar looked baffled.

"Why do you say that?" Dr. Greenfield asked interestedly. He didn't say someone else had taken the owl, and Tammy and I kept quiet. Anybody who was putting on Mr. Farrar had our blessing.

"Well—uh—Kleeman was so positive—and it was the one thing Miss Alston needed to convince her about her niece. Look, I really have got to get down to the office. We'll have another meeting tonight, if Dr. Alston wants to." And he drove off.

Dr. Greenfield strolled around the workshop part of the garage. "Hm. Copper sulphate. Wonder what he's been making."

"That's poison," Tammy said.

"I know, dear," her father said.

"Well?" I could hardly wait. "Don't you want to know, Tam, how I guessed about how Kleeman knew what to tell Dr. Alston?"

"Sure," Tammy said obligingly. "How'd you guess?"

"Well, after your father said what he did about finding out where Dame Pythia got the information that nobody could possibly know but the victim, it just came to me. It was simple. Who was the only other person who knew Miranda when she was a baby? And Miss Judith had said Miranda's mother was interested in psychic things. So naturally she might be trying to get in touch with her in The Other World, and might have met members of the Psychic Society at that convention in New York. And Mr. Farrar and Dame Pythia could have gone back and found out anything they wanted to know, by asking her questions while pretending to tell her things that came from Miranda. That was what I was trying to remember about the desk—it had the books in it, remember, that Miranda's mother had given her. Her mother was the clue to the whole thing."

"Dr. Alston will be glad to know there's a rational explanation," Dr. Greenfield said.

"But Miss Judith will be disappointed."

"And it was clever of you to get Mr. Farrar to admit he knew Miranda's mother, Lindsey."

"Any time," I said airily. "That trick always works. Even on Eddie."

"But," Tammy said, "the cement owl still isn't explained."

"It isn't even found."

We went back across the street. "I'd better check in at home," I said, "and let them know I'm still alive. And see what Sherry and Eddie and Kirk are up to. Want to come, Tammy?"

"Might as well."

"Shall I," said Dr. Greenfield, "tell the Alstons what you deduced, Lindsey? Or would you rather tell them yourself?"

"Oh, please, you tell them, sir. I hate to see how disappointed Miss Judith is going to be. But if only we could find the owl—you see, I have a theory, Dr. Greenfield, that maybe Miranda really is hanging around, although not bothering with Kleeman and Dame Pythia and Mr. Farrar. But maybe she stays close to Miss Judith, because she loves her. If I could come back after I die, I wouldn't haunt just any old strangers, and I wouldn't show up at séances like Dame Pythia's—I'd stick around close to the people I loved when I was alive. Maybe Miranda wants us to find the cement owl and show it to Miss Judith for her birthday, just like Miranda meant to do herself. And then maybe she could rest in peace."

"It's a fine theory," Dr. Greenfield said solemnly. "Let me know if you find anything to substantiate it. Well, I'll go tell the Alston's there's nothing to the 'evidential.' "

We saw the three kids down by the rabbit cages, and they turned around quickly when they saw us; so we knew they were up to something.

All at once I had an inspiration. Maybe the psychological trick would work in a slightly different form, on Sherry, too.

"Sherry," I said casually, "how did you know where to dig for the cement owl, last night?"

She opened her mouth to answer, and then caught herself and clammed up. But Eddie blurted out, "Miranda told her!"

"Yep," Kirk said.

So she did have it. Where had she hidden it? But—Miranda?

Sherry smiled confidingly then, glancing up from under those witch-bangs. "Yes. Of course. She told me where it was."

"You're putting us on," Tammy said flatly.

"Oh, no, Tammy. I wouldn't do that." Sherry was the picture of innocence.

"If you dug it up," I said, "where is it now?"

"Miranda doesn't want me to tell anybody. She wants me to wait and show it to Aunt Judith on her birthday."

Well, there it was. It still sounded as if Sherry really had been in communication with Miranda's ghost. And there was no real evidence that she had ever actually found Miranda's diary, although personally I felt absolutely certain she had. It was the only way she could have known most of the things she knew. But Miss Judith had said she was sure Miranda didn't tell in the diary where she had hidden the owl.

Sherry said, "I've got to go now."

Kirk and Eddie started to follow her, but I said sternly, "It's nearly lunch time. You two go inside and wash up," and they—for a wonder—obeyed me. But Sherry turned around and made a funny sign in the air with her arms, like crossing her heart in the air, and ended with her fingers on her lips, and Eddie and Kirk imitated it. I guess that meant they had sworn to keep her secrets. They kept looking at the rabbits and giggling; so I guessed the secrets had something to do with Brer and Mrs. Brer as well as with the cement owl.

I walked around to the front with Tammy as she was leaving, and we saw Dr. Alston and Dr. Greenfield come out of the Alstons' house, and Dr. Alston went striding over to the Farrars' looking furious—and then in a few minutes he came back and shook hands with Dr. Greenfield, and they each went on inside their own houses.

Tammy and I kept on watching the Farrars' to see what would happen, and sure enough, a taxi drove up and Dame Pythia rushed out of the house and got into it. That was the last we ever saw of Dame Pythia. Too bad. We don't get to see a medium perform her tricks every day. There never was a word of publicity in the papers about her giving a sitting for the famous scientist, Dr. Alston, either. She was an awful fake. But still, I'd like to see a true medium sometime—one of those who really are honestly psychic. I'd like to go to a séance that's for real, not phony.

After lunch Tammy came over, and we were walking out into the backyard when Eddie said for no good reason, "You girls mustn't bother Brer."

"Well, that's a new one," I said, and Tammy added, "Who's bothering your old rabbit?"

"Wait a minute," I said. "Why not, Eddie? Brer kind of likes to be taken out of his cage and petted. Not that I have time to pet any rabbits today."

Eddie—too late—saw that he had made me suspicious, and tried to change the subject. "I think I'll train Eight for a house-rabbit," he said quickly. "It ought to be pretty easy to housebreak a rabbit, huh, Lin? Easier than a puppy. Will you help me? Will you ask Mama to let me have Eight for a house-rabbit, please, Lin?" When Eddie looks at you with those soulful blue eyes of his, it's hard not to promise him anything. But I resisted. If there's anything we don't need while Mama's pregnant, it's the job of housebreaking a rabbit.

"Never mind about Eight," I said. "It's Brer we were talking about. Why don't you want us to bother him?"

"Well, because he's a new father," Eddie said after thinking awhile. "New fathers get disturbed pretty easy. I wouldn't want him disturbed."

"Don't worry—we wouldn't think of disturbing him," I said, giving Tammy a significant pressure on the arm as we walked away around the corner of the house. "That is, not until they've gone over to the Alstons' and out of sight of the cages," I told her. "Then we'll see what it is they've got hidden in Brer's cage!"

It seemed as though they would never go. They had to clean the cages and put fresh hay in—lots of fresh hay, much more than usual. We were watching from behind the hydrangea bushes at the corner of the house. "See, they're hiding something in there, behind all that hay," I guessed. Then they had to fill the water pans and get some lettuce leaves from Mama for the rabbits' lunch, and pet each one individually, and clean up the old hay they had spilled on the ground.

But at last the boys started over to Sherry's. As

soon as we saw her let them in the door, we hurried over to the cages.

We could hardly see Brer at all, for the piles of hay they had put in there with him. But I held him, with one hand soothingly on his back, while I scrambled in the hay with the other hand, and Tammy felt around with both hers.

"Feel anything?" I asked.

"Only hay." Tammy sneezed.

"I believe I do!" Yes, it was something that didn't belong in the corner of a rabbit cage. Something hard and heavy, like a rock. Like a cement owl.

"Here it is, Tammy!"

I pulled it out. It looked more like a lump of cement than anything else, but it definitely had golden eyes—the yellow glass marbles—and there were feathered wings outlined with a nail or something before the cement hardened, the way the boys had told us it was made. And you could see the owl-shaped head and curved beak, if you knew what to look for.

Both of us looked eagerly into the golden eyes. How did Miranda put love in its eyes?

As far as we could see, there wasn't any. They were just yellow glass marbles.

Tammy said, "What did she mean, love in its eyes?"

"I don't know. But—" I said slowly, "do you

suppose she meant—you know, what's the word
—figuratively speaking? Not actually? Could she
have meant because she loved Miss Judith and
Miss Judith loved her, the owl they made would
have love in its eyes whenever either of them
looked at it?"

"We'll have to ask Miss Judith."

"But we don't want her to see the owl till her
birthday, do we?"

"Well, hide it again, so Sherry won't know we
found it." We tucked it back in the straw, and
then ran over to Alstons'. By that time Sherry and

136

the boys were out in the yard; so we went in to see Miss Judith.

She was in her room, and called to us to come on up. She looked as if she had been crying. Miss Judith is the only lady we know who always looks dignified even after she's been crying.

"We're sorry Dame Pythia was a fraud, Miss Judith," I said. "But you know, we still might find the owl for you. Miranda still might be around. Just because they used some phony stuff trying to fool Dr. Alston doesn't necessarily mean that something real might not have come through from Miranda's spirit anyhow, in spite of them. Maybe the owl was really buried there."

Tammy said, "Miss Judith, please tell us how that owl had love in its eyes? Was it just the kind only you and Miranda could see—the figurative kind—or could anybody see it? Could Lindsey and I see it—if we found the owl?"

"Have you found it?" Miss Judith asked excitedly.

"Not exactly," I said cautiously. "But we need to know about the love in its eyes, in case we should run across a cement owl."

"Well, I'll tell you. Yes, it really was love—the word 'love' was scratched in very small letters with a stylus in the wet cement in each eye socket, and filled in with green paint so the letters would show up, before we put the clear yellow glass marbles in. We put the marbles in very carefully so the letters wouldn't blur, and the paint had dried quicker than the cement. That was still wet; so the marbles stuck all right. It looked wonderful."

I looked at Tammy, and Tammy looked at me. We both said at the same time, "It's the wrong owl!"

11

THE GHOST
RIDES AWAY

"The question is, does Sherry know it's the wrong one?" Tammy said.

"I don't think she does."

"If she does, that means she's putting us on, about Miranda telling her to dig there."

"But if she doesn't know it's the wrong one," I said, "how did she know where to dig at all? For that matter, even if she does know it's the wrong one, how'd she know it was *there?*"

"What are you two talking about?" Miss Judith asked.

"Miss Judith, just trust us," I said earnestly. "All we know is, Sherry dug up the owl that was buried on the bank of the pond. But we think it's the wrong owl. As far as we could tell, it doesn't have love in its eyes. Of course," I said thoughtfully, "we ought to take another look. Not knowing exactly what to look for, we might have missed it. There might have been dirt over the letters or something. Now that we know, we can tell in a minute."

"Where is it?" Miss Judith said. "I could tell at a glance."

"Miranda wanted you to see it on your birthday," I told her. "We thought we might be able to find it and surprise you by showing you where she hid it, on your birthday, and then her Unquiet Spirit could rest. If that's what she wants. Wouldn't you rather wait, in case we do find the real owl?"

Miss Judith surprised us. "No," she said. "If you find the real one, I'd like to have it at once. Because that's not what Miranda wants—if she wants anything. She wants to be recognized, that's all. She wants her father to be proud to say, 'I once had another dear little girl; her name was Miranda.' If you bring me the real owl, I'll put it on the mantel with her picture, and tell everybody that Miranda and I made the owl. It may not have any effect on Miranda's spirit, but I know it'll make me feel a whole lot less guilty."

"But what about Sherry?" I said, and then wished I hadn't.

"What do you mean, child? What about Sherry?"

"Well, we have a theory that maybe Sherry's jealous of Miranda. If somehow she found out—or just guessed—how you loved Miranda, she might think your teaching her to knit isn't as good as teaching Miranda to make a blue rose or a cement owl. Sherry might be feeling sort of left out too." I wasn't saying it very well, but Miss Judith got the message. She looked troubled.

"I see," she murmured, half to herself. "The poor wistful child. I've been unfair to her, too. How could I?"

"Well," Tammy said briskly to me, because it felt awkward to look at Miss Judith right then, the way she was feeling, "let's try to find out how Sherry knew where to dig, and take another look at that owl, and if it's not the real one—I'm pretty sure it's not—then we must find the real one. We've got our work cut out for us."

"Bring me the one Sherry dug up," Miss Judith said.

"We didn't want her to know yet that we found it."

"Why didn't we?" Tammy asked me.

"I don't know exactly," I admitted frankly. "It just seemed like it might be a kind of psychological advantage."

That reminded me of my psychological trick, and I said, "Maybe it'll work on Eddie again—the trap. He might give something away. If we can get him alone—without Sherry, I mean. Good-bye, Miss Judith. We'll let you know what happens."

Luck was with us. Eddie and Kirk were in their room, and Sherry wasn't with them. "Where's Sherry?" I asked.

"She's gone to ask her Dad again to get her a

horse for her birthday. She thinks he might slip up and promise while her mother's away. She'll be back in a few minutes."

We hung around, tickling Kirk and rough-housing with him a little, until Eddie was lying on his stomach on the floor, absorbed in a comic book. I've noticed that when he's doing something like reading a comic book, he sometimes answers a question automatically without thinking exactly what he's saying, but he answers right. It comes out of his subconscious mind, Tammy says. So I asked him, very casually, "Eddie, was it before or after Miranda told her where to dig for the cement owl that Sherry actually found out where it was?"

He answered absent-mindedly, without looking up from Captain Astro, "Before. We didn't know what it was, though, that we saw Mr. Farrar burying there, till Miranda told her."

"You haven't brushed your teeth since lunch," I said, to leave him something else in his subconscious mind to remember that we talked about, and Tammy and I left very quietly, so as not to disturb him. In the hall after we shut the door we hugged each other in silent congratulation, and then rushed down the stairs and outside.

"Mr. Farrar!" I exclaimed. "We might have known. But how—?"

"Remember the day he came by when we were hunting for the owl and the boys told him how it was made?" Tammy said. "He was very much interested in all the details."

"Let's go tell your father," I said. "Even with Dame Pythia out, he'll want to know about Mr. Farrar making a fake owl and burying it."

Dr. Greenfield listened, nodding. "What did it look like? Very old? Or as if it had just been made?"

"Oh, it looked old, all right. It might have been buried for years. All green and moldy, with dirt clinging to it," I said. "Of course, the hole by the pond was pretty muddy—red clay mud."

"That's what he was doing with the copper sulphate," Dr. Greenfield said. "It would give a greenish-blue tinge to the cement, and if he mixed it with red clay or dirt or old green moss and rubbed it in before it was quite dry—yes, it could look old, all right."

"And remember, Tammy, before the séance we saw Mr. Farrar going out the back way toward Alstons' and then coming back the front way. Just before all the people arrived. I bet that was when he went to bury it, knowing the Alstons were already here, and probably thinking Sherry was at our house. But the kids were watching him and went right behind him and dug it up."

"But you say he didn't get the eyes right?" Dr. Greenfield asked.

"That's what we've got to be sure of," Tammy said. "We're going to take another look, now. Of course he didn't know about love in its eyes. And it wasn't in the diary, I suppose. Sherry might or might not have the diary—I guess we'll never know. But anyhow, she doesn't know about the eyes either, whether she has it or not. So she doesn't recognize that it's the wrong owl. And Miranda's ghost never told her where to dig. She must have just told Eddie and Kirk afterward that Miranda said so."

I hated to give up our ghost, though it did sound improbable. "But still, if Sherry doesn't have the diary she must really have been in communication with Miranda about some of those other things. And if by any chance she does turn out to know about the right owl with love in its eyes, then she must have found out from Miranda."

"Let me know," Dr. Greenfield said.

"She does have the diary somewhere," Tammy said with conviction. "She might even be keeping it with her all the time—that's why we can't find it. Sometimes I've seen her putting her hand against her belt—you know, the way you'd do if you were being sure something you had underneath there was secure."

"That would explain it," I admitted. "But we don't know for sure. And she might be smart enough to destroy it, so we never would know."

"Then there's the chance she might find the right owl purely by accident," Tammy said.

We reconnoitered. The coast was clear—the kids weren't at the rabbit cages, but we couldn't spot them anywhere else either. We should have known better than to count on their not seeing us. Just as I pulled the owl out of Brer's cage, and started to rub the dust off its glass eyes, Sherry came tearing around the corner of the house, with the boys panting after her.

"Quick, Tammy!" I said. "Do you see any love?" I held it out and we both looked, but couldn't see anything except cement behind the dingy yellow glass.

Then Sherry swooped in like a whirlwind. "Give me that owl!" she shouted. "Don't you dare take it! I'm the one who's going to give it to Aunt Judith for her birthday, so she'll—" She snatched it out of my hand and ran, and I couldn't tell if she was sobbing or laughing.

Tammy and I ran after her, even though we knew now it was the wrong owl, because you can't let a smaller child think she has gotten the best of you. Especially, you can't let your kid brothers think some younger girl can get the best of their older sister, or you'd never have any control over them again.

Sherry could really run! And when she got to the big old magnolia tree, she proved she could climb, too. She was going up so fast we couldn't catch her, though we're fast climbers, and Tammy and I were afraid she would wiggle onto the roof and into the window of her own room where we'd never get her.

Evidently she didn't think of that. She went right on past her window, on up high, just above the attic window. Even from where we were, the ground seemed so far away that I felt dizzy. I said, "Tammy, what if she should fall? It would be our fault."

"You mean for chasing her? Yes, I guess we'd better not make her go any higher," Tammy agreed, after she looked down too, and tightened her grip around the big trunk of the tree. It was good to have something solid to hold onto. Sometimes where the limbs joined the trunk there were holes you could catch your fingers into—holes that squirrels or woodpeckers had used for nests.

"Look, Sherry," I called, "stop climbing. You're going too high. Stop climbing!"

"You can't make me!" Sherry called back. "This is my tree now. It used to be hers. She climbed as high as she wanted to, and I can go higher than she could. I've been up this high lots of times. So have Eddie and Kirk." I made a mental note to tell Dad about that, though it was probably a big fat lie.

"Why don't you level with us, Sherry?" Tammy said reasonably. "You know you're just pretending about Miranda, but you've got Miss Judith all worried. You don't mean to hurt Miss Judith, do you? She loves you."

There was a silence. Then Sherry said, "Not as much as she loved Miranda."

146

"Yes, she does," I said. "It's just different. Nobody loves two people exactly the same way. Think it through, Sherry; you don't love your mother exactly the same way you do your father, do you? But you wouldn't say you love one of them the most, would you? You love them differently. That's the way it is with Miss Judith about you and Miranda."

Sherry didn't answer, but I hoped I'd gotten through to her—that she was thinking it over. I went on trying to persuade her. "Come on down, now, before one of us falls and gets hurt. Okay?"

"You won't try to get this owl away from me?"

"No. We don't want that old owl. It's the wrong owl, anyhow—don't you know that?"

She looked down at us suspiciously. She was astride a big leafy limb just above us, as if she were riding Nightmare. The sun made lights and shadows all around us in a sort of shiny-dark-green, black-and-white world. Sherry had the owl in her hand; all that time she had been climbing with one hand, and was still holding on with it, and when I looked down at the ground I shuddered. It really was a terribly tall tree—taller than the two-story-and-attic house.

Now Sherry looked at the owl suspiciously, as if she could see by looking, why it was the wrong one. Then she decided we wouldn't have said it without a good reason, so she went along with what we'd said. "I know it's the wrong one. Miranda

147

told me." She flung it to the ground, and I screamed, "Look out!" in case Eddie or Kirk had happened to be standing there. The owl made a *Chunk* sound as it hit the ground.

"She told me where the right one is, too," Sherry said, in a different sort of voice.

Tammy and I both saw it just as she said that.

There was a squirrel hole almost at Sherry's back, where another limb branched out, but she could see into it when she turned her head. And we could see into it when we looked up at a certain angle. It was simply a round hole, just big enough to form a perfect niche. For a cement owl. With golden eyes.

It was there. I thought for a minute I was imagining it, but no. It was really there. Tammy said, "Look!" in an awed sort of voice. Miranda must have meant for Miss Judith to look out the attic window and see the surprise—Miss Judith could never have climbed that tree, not even thirteen years ago when she was younger.

"Sherry," I said excitedly, "does that one have love in its eyes?"

Did she hesitate a minute? Did she look before she answered? We couldn't tell. But she said, "Yes."

"Then it's the right one."

We stared up at her, and she looked back at us, defying us to touch it. She even let go of the limb and folded her arms and looked down at us with

her chin out, like an arrogant little imp. I wondered how to handle her psychologically.

"Sherry," I said persuasively, "why don't you take that owl, the one Miranda made, and give it to Miss Judith? We don't want it, but Miss Judith does. And she'd love you more than anything in the world if you brought it to her."

"More than she loved Miranda?"

"Differently," I said firmly.

Sherry went back to her fantasy bit. "Miranda wants me to show it to Aunt Judith on her birthday."

"But your Aunt Judith wants it now. She told us so. She doesn't want to wait till her birthday. You can tell her it's an advance birthday present. From you."

Sherry said slowly, "I guess—I will, then."

So we all came down from the tree, and Tammy and I went home, and left Sherry to make up to Miss Judith.

After supper, when we went back over there, Miss Judith had Sherry's picture on one end of the living room mantel and Miranda's on the other, and the owl in the middle. And I thought Dr. Alston looked happier than I'd ever seen him, sitting there holding Mrs. Alston's hand. Instead of the usual lamps, there were lighted candles in the sconces, just like a party.

Miss Judith told us, "Girls, here's the owl my niece Miranda made, with love in its eyes. My dear little niece Sherry found it and gave it to me, for a birthday present." And she smiled at Sherry, and Sherry snuggled up to her, and I could guess who might get a horse for her birthday, if Miss Judith could manage it.

The candlelight left the corners of the room dim, and I felt sort of shivery-happy, as if Miranda had come to the party too. But I couldn't see anything except shadows, hovering around the edges. I was asking silently, Is there—anybody—there? It was no use to listen for *The Dance of the Fireflies* because the piano was right in the room with us, and it was shut.

I wondered why I felt so curiously on the edge of expecting something else to happen, something mysterious and—and about Miranda. But not really sad because she wasn't any longer a girl like us. Just—well, like Shakespeare said, what had happened to Miranda was just *a sea-change into something rich and strange*.

There was nobody else in the house; there couldn't have been. We were all in the livingroom—but I thought I heard something, and felt a little breeze go past me, light and cool.

And it must have blown through the hall, too, because I heard a door softly and finally closing.

And I thought I heard a horse's hoofs, very far off, and then fading out to silence.

But of course it was just my imagination. It had

to be. Tammy said later that she hadn't noticed anything at all.

Miss Judith was waiting for us to admire the owl. So we did. And I winked at Sherry, but she didn't wink back. Then I saw that she was crying.

"Why, what's the matter, Sherry?" Miss Judith said, and she hugged Sherry, with a lot of love in the hug. "What are you crying about?"

"Oh, Aunt Judith," Sherry sniffled, "she's gone away and I'll never see her again. She said so. She rode away on Nightmare and she's never coming back."

The Alstons have gone back to Houston now, and Miss Judith goes to the Garden Club instead of the Psychic Society, and Sherry writes to Eddie once in a while and he answers. The other day when we were all talking, Tammy said, "Well, I think she made it all up, after she found the diary. I don't believe she ever saw Miranda at all."

Eddie said loyally, "I do. I believe she could see Miranda, even if we couldn't."

"Yep," Kirk said.

Tammy said, "What do you think, Lindsey? Was there a ghost next door?"

All I could say was, "I don't know."

Because I really don't.